A CERTAIN BLINDNESS

In the eyes of solicitor Eric Ward there was something odd about Arthur Egan's life and death. Egan's estate comprised a large sum, to go to an heir no one knew he had. Egan had served a term for manslaughter committed during an armed robbery of Lord Morcomb's estate. Indications were that the evidence against him had been planted. The present Lord Morcomb was facing heavy death duties, and Ward's firm had to advise how these could be handled. Despite warnings from the senior partner that he was wasting time on the Egan estate, Ward persisted – and his investigation soon led to murder.

A CERTAIN BLINDNESS

A CERTAIN BLINDNESS

by

Roy Lewis

Magna Large Print Books
Long Preston, North Yorkshire,
BD23 4ND, England.

British Library Cataloguing in Publication Data.

Lewis, Roy
    A certain blindness.

    A catalogue record of this book is
    available from the British Library

    ISBN   978-0-7505-4131-2

First published in Great Britain by
Templar North Publishing Ltd.

Copyright © Roy Lewis 1980 and 2011

Cover illustration © Tony Watson by arrangement with
Arcangel Images

Magna Large Print is an imprint of Library Magna Books Ltd.

Printed and bound in Great Britain by
T.J. (International) Ltd., Cornwall, PL28 8RW

11880738

Chapter One

1

The pain came for him again, cat claws
scratching at the back of his eyeballs, ex-
quisite darts of agony searing through his
head, and he stumbled to his feet, reaching
into the desk drawer for the bottle of fluid.
The washroom lay at the end of the corridor,
and he lurched through the doorway as the
sharp lances ripped at the tissue of his eyes.
He gripped the bottle tightly in his hand and
opened the door of the washroom, locked it
behind him and the cat was stretching,
hungrily, unsheathing its claws again as he
peered through a red haze at the phial,
twisted off the top, inserted the dropper and
brought up a quantity of the pilocarpine.
Head back, he allowed the fluid to drip
into the corner of his eye and his nerve ends
screamed with pain as the tension increased.
The light was dim in the washroom – he had
not turned on the light – and he closed his
eyes, put his head back against the wall. His

hands were trembling; it would not be long before the shuddering began, part hysteria, part pain. It wouldn't last long; he knew that from experience. But while it did, it was so *unacceptable*. In a sense, it was worse than the pain, his body's reaction. It denoted a weakness he refused to recognize in himself, and yet it was there, every time.

As he stood there, waiting for the attack to pass, he could remember George Knox's hands. He had been surprised by their softness and their deftness, for Knox was a heavy, awkward man with a snarling voice. But as Knox had moved his face under the light his fingers had been as light as a woman's.

'How long have you been having these headaches?' he had asked.

'Hell, I don't know. Months, I suppose.'

'Not very specific, for a jack.'

'What I mean is, I've always been a *bit* bothered, but who isn't, with the kind of paperwork and overtime we do?'

'But more severe of late?' Knox had asked quietly.

'You could say that.'

'Worse during the day, or night?'

'Night, usually.'

'Hmmm. But your vision *has* been impaired, hasn't it? And there have been occasions when your eyelids have been red and swollen. And at night ... lights seem to have coloured haloes around them.'

'I didn't tell you that!'

'You didn't need to. Any more than you need to tell me you've noticed a certain greenish discolouration of the iris, and a hardness about your eyeballs. They're classical symptoms, along with headaches, pain in the eyes, nausea and vomiting at night–'

'Symptoms of what?'

'Glaucoma,' George Knox had said, simply. There had been more, later. A lecture, almost, on how glaucoma was caused by the pressure of fluids within the eye – local congestion pushing the iris forward until it blocked the canal of Schlemm at its junction with the cornea, where the fluids normally escaped. Knox had told him how there was the possibility that the pressure could build up until it eventually destroyed the ends of the optic nerves. He'd also explained how acute glaucoma could be treated by iridectomy: the removal of a small section of the iris, allowing the fluid to escape. And in the case of chronic glaucoma a filtration procedure was possible to establish a new drainage path for the fluid.

And then, finally, the diagnosis.

'*Chronic* glaucoma, I'm afraid. That means the results of surgery would be less than certain. And it also means an immediate discharge from the Force.'

Eric Ward peered in the washroom mirror. His eyelids were swollen and red, but the pain was easing. After a little while he washed his face in cold water, and made his way back to his room.

There was a certain irony in it all, he thought as he sat down behind his desk and pulled the volume of Halsbury's *Statutes* towards him. He had reached a turning point in his career with the Force. In his own time he had struggled through a law degree, part-time at the polytechnic, and had toyed with the idea of leaving the police. And Knox had told him that tension, strain, overwork had exacerbated the illness. What he had thought was the result of reading lawbooks late into the night, combined with a great deal of work as a detective-inspector, had in reality been something different – the worsening of an illness that Knox claimed could have been dealt with more easily, earlier – an operation to reduce the tension on the nerve ends. But now, he had his law degree, glaucoma, a

10

pension at forty and no job.

So the decision was, in a sense, made for him. A few approaches to law firms in Newcastle, and finally an offer from Francis, Shaw and Elder. With his degree he'd need to undertake an articled clerkship for two years, and complete his Law Society Finals, and though he was rather old to start a career as a solicitor, well, there were clients who didn't care to have their cases handled by young fledglings.

Joseph Francis, the senior partner in the firm had put that rather nicely, in fact, and had seemed to understand some of the problems that Eric Ward faced personally in making this change. He had showed little understanding in placing Eric under the control of his son, Paul Francis, however. But then, what man knew his own son well?

Ward frowned, rubbed his eyes gently, and read again sections 48 to 56 of the Mines and Quarries Act 1954. He'd promised to get the papers to Paul Francis before three o'clock so he'd have half an hour with them before the client claiming compensation called for advice on his projected action against the National Coal Board. How had he described himself? A 'market man' – an experienced underground worker who had trained in different types of underground working.

It wasn't a bad description for an articled clerk, either, Ward thought sourly. You worked at a whole range of things, underground, for a pittance, while the solicitor supervising your articles took the fruits of your work and charged fees at his own rates. If only young Francis did it more graciously.

He shook his head, replaced the bottle of pilocarpine in his desk, and applied himself with more assiduity to the market man's complaint against the safety measures taken in his pit.

'Section 52,' he wrote, 'states that no person shall withdraw support from the roof or sides of any place in a mine otherwise than by a method or device by which he does so from a position of safety...'

At three o'clock precisely he had finished the report and made his way along to the office on the first floor occupied by Paul Francis.

2

The junior partner in Francis, Shaw and Elder knew about Eric Ward's glaucoma; they all did in the office. But it was not something he could easily handle.

Sympathy was out of the question, expressed or unexpressed – this was a business and there was no place for sentiment. Money had to be made and every man must pull his weight.

Not that Ward didn't pull his weight; indeed, after a year as an articled clerk he had learned so fast that he effectively operated as another assistant solicitor, only occasionally requiring advice and assistance. He could work largely unsupervised, but in a sense that rather nettled Paul Francis. He was unable to rationalize his irritation; not that he tried very hard. It was a compound of several things: the vague sense of insecurity he felt in Eric Ward's presence; a feeling of intellectual inferiority because of his own lack of a degree; the calm, phlegmatic manner in which Ward refused to react to slights; the efficient manner in which he discharged the numerous tasks that Paul Francis thrust upon him. And then there was the older man's physical presence. Against Ward's six feet, Paul was very conscious of his own slightly built five-feet-seven frame. Nor did Ward move like the archetypal policeman: he was a big man, but still lean and soft-moving, light on his feet.

And clients liked him. It was perhaps the

most irritating thing of all – on the occasions when Paul Francis had allowed Ward to remain with him when interviewing the client, somehow the *control* had always seemed to pass to the ex-policeman.

No, Paul Francis thought as Eric Ward entered his room, it isn't the most irritating thing about him, after all. What really niggles is that Ward knows, he bloody well *knows* what I think about him.

'Have you got the report?' Paul Francis asked, glancing at his watch as though to check the time of arrival of the file. It might, on the other hand, be his usual initial nervousness when Ward entered his room.

'Yes, it's here.' Ward placed the file on Francis's desk and then walked across to stand near the window, leaning against the radiator as Francis picked up the file and began to read it. He knew the young solicitor would want to discuss it, as soon as he had got tired of reading, ploughing through the detailed authorities Ward had raised. He folded his arms, and waited. The pain in his eyes had receded now and while the redness of his eyelids remained, the puffiness had also disappeared.

'So what do you think, then?' Francis asked, riffling through the sheets in the file.

14

'I think your client has a case. From what I can see of the facts he raises, the Board could well be in breach of statutory duty under section 53 of the 1954 Act.'

'His injuries came from a fall,' Paul Francis muttered. 'What about the manager?'

'I take it from the authorities that a manager is not automatically guilty of a contravention if a fall occurs, but a fall itself is evidence of some breach.'

'We'll take counsel's opinion, of course,' Paul Francis said.

'Of course.' Ward smiled inwardly. Francis had made the statement as though to suggest some doubt as to Ward's checking of authorities. In fact, it was old Joe Francis's dictum within the firm that on any case of difficulty or magnitude counsel's opinion was *always* to be taken. It was the obvious way to avoid any claim of negligence – pass the burden to a barrister, who couldn't be sued, and charge the client extra for doing it. It always amused Ward: the client paid extra for the privilege of being unable thereafter to sue.

'Okay,' Paul said, tossing the file aside and leaning back in his chair. 'Give me a quick rundown on the authorities and the advice you suggest.' Ward did so, smoothly and easily, relying largely on *Cough v National*

Coal Board and *Stein v O'Hanlon,* and grimly amused at the irritation in Paul Francis's narrow features as Ward made no check of the file itself.

'Right, Eric,' Paul Francis said when he had finished, 'the client will be in to see me in about half an hour, and I'll go over these papers now. You needn't stay. What have you got on your desk at the moment?'

'Couple of conveyances. Two county court matters. A few other things which—'

'Yeah, all right,' Francis interrupted him as though he had hardly heard him. 'Well, look, I'm pretty snowed under right now, so there's a couple of things you can relieve me of. One of them is a big one, and we'll have to work in harness over it. Joe—' he always referred to his father as Joe, though not in his presence – 'Joe will be handling it in person, probably, but will want the background work dealt with before the next series of meetings. Ah ... here it is.'

As he spoke he had been rustling papers in the large wooden filing cabinet beside his desk. Now he extracted a bulky file tied with pink ribbon, and weighed it thoughtfully for a few moments before passing it to Ward. 'As you can see, it's a pretty hefty matter.'

There were dates written in Joe Francis's

16

spidery hand on the cover. Ward looked at them, and frowned. 'This been running for six years?'

'Seems so. And while Joe's been handling it, he doesn't regard estate duty as his strong suit, exactly. He was being backed up by Robinson, you know, but since *he's* set up as a partner in Northampton, Joe's been left a bit high and dry. Which is how we come in.'

Eric Ward nodded, understanding. Father and son had that much in common at least. Joe Francis might be a sound lawyer, but he still liked to have someone else to do the work for him, while he fronted with the client. Ward looked at the name on the cover of the file: *Morcomb v Inland Revenue Commissioners*. A six-year run, already. Soothing bedtime reading, no doubt.

'All right, I'll get started on this tomorrow morning, once I've cleared those conveyances.'

Ward turned to go, but Francis was back at the filing cabinet again. 'Hold on, don't go yet. There's another one I'd like you to deal with. The Morcomb file is due for discussion early next week when Lord Morcomb—'

'*Lord* Morcomb?'

Paul Francis sniffed, managed a grin. 'Oh yes, we get the best kind of clients here, you know. His lordship is leaving his North-umberland estates to pay us a visit next week – unless he calls us out there – so you'll need to hone up that file, then meet me for a discussion on Friday. But first, you'd better get hold of this thing. It's been on my conscience, a bit.'

Ward took the file held out to him. On the cover was stated, simply, EGAN, ARTHUR *(deceased)*.

Back in his own office, Eric Ward received a cup of tea gratefully from the typist/recep-tionist who trebled up as his secretarial assistance, and opened the Egan file. A quick glance showed him why the file had been on Paul Francis's conscience. It must have been sitting in his filing cabinet for weeks – maybe two months – and nothing had been done about it. Details on the file were scant and it looked like a simple administration matter, but though Francis could have dealt with it fairly quickly it was obvious it had been thrust aside as relatively unimportant. Fees for completing an estate administration on intestacy were not high – though Joseph Francis held the view that all fees were fees, and not to be sneezed at.

Ward sipped his tea, checked the address

18

given in the file. Westerhope. That was useful. It was more or less on the way to Wylam, where Eric Ward had bought a small house near the river, and he could conveniently call on the way back this evening, take a look at the property, see what had or had not been done. He pushed the file to one side and picked up the Morcomb file, undid the pink ties, and started at the beginning. Ten minutes' reading and he fanned through the papers to later stages, then pulled a face.

It was going to be heavy work, and he could understand why Paul Francis would want a resume. And Joseph Francis, too. The valuation of a landed estate in Northumberland, and a barrage of arguments based on readings of the dreaded Finance Acts. He scowled, and finished his tea.

At least, he could say he'd be getting a fine training at Francis, Shaw and Elder, even if it was very much sink or swim.

He closed the file, retied the tapes and got to work on the conveyances. Yet as he worked for the next hour or so his mind kept drifting away in a manner uncharacteristic of him. There was something fluttering at the back of his mind, an echo, a whisper he could not place or define. He leaned back in his chair, stretched, came back again and tried to concentrate, succeeding for a while, but the niggling puzzle returned, unformed, shapeless as a thought, but there in his mind.

It was five-thirty before he finished the work already on his desk. He put the Morcomb file in his filing cabinet, to look at first thing in the morning, and then rose, empty cup in one hand, the administration file he was taking home with him in the other.

It was only after he had returned the cup and walked out to his car that he knew what was bothering him. He got into the car, turned on the ignition, then glanced again at the file lying on the passenger seat.

Arthur Egan.

Somewhere, he had come across that name before.

3

The traffic was fairly heavy in town, as usual, but he avoided the centre, driving up through Gosforth, then cutting across Town Moor until he reached the Jedburgh road. Past the Cowgate roundabout it was only a matter of minutes to Westerhope, and he had no difficulty finding the house. One enquiry of a woman emerging from an off-licence with curlers under her headscarf and beer bottles in her shopping-bag sent him into two left turns, and he found himself in Kitchener Avenue.

No. 17 was an unpretentious, red-brick, semi-detached house near the curve in the avenue; there was a green, carefully painted gate barring access to unwelcome visitors, and Ward was surprised to note that the tiny garden and hedge in front of the house had been carefully kept, even though Egan had been dead for several months. He frowned, hesitated, fingering the key in his pocket. According to the file, there was no one living in the house. He opened the garden gate, walked up to the front door and rang the bell.

The peal echoed inside the house. As if in immediate response the door of the next house opened and a small, stocky woman with bright, needle-sharp blue eyes looked at him over the hedge. 'No one in, hinny. Old man died some time back. House is empty now, like.'

Ward nodded, smiling slightly and produced the key from his pocket, inserted it into the lock. The woman next door raised her eyebrows. 'Hey, what you doin'?'

'I'm from Francis, Shaw and Elder, the

solicitors,' Ward explained. 'We're dealing with the estate.'

She stared at him as though legal gentlemen were beyond her experience or understanding. 'I'm Mrs Towers,' she said defensively. 'I was his neighbour.'

Ward nodded, accepting this self-evident fact and then stepped into the narrow passageway. It was cool and dim inside, and there was a fusty smell in the house, damp and disuse already marking the atmosphere. The stairs stretched up ahead of him; to the left was a small sitting room, the door ajar; ahead of him a kitchen in which there was also a table from which the old man had obviously taken his meals. Ward placed the file on the table and commenced an inspection of the house.

He was somewhat surprised that Paul Francis had not yet arranged for an estate agent to clear the furniture and sell it by auction – not that there was much there to sell. A three-piece suite, two bedrooms furnished, but one obviously hardly used, a quiet spartan living, it would seem. On the other hand, maybe Paul had done nothing because of the letter.

A strange note, and an unusual one to bring the firm into the administration.

When he returned to the kitchen again he picked up the file and extracted the letter. It had been found in Egan's bedside locker at the hospital, after he had died. Ward read it again, now.

'I have every respect for the professional integrity of the firm of Francis, Shaw and Elder. In the event of my death I wish them to administer my estate. If my only child remains unprovided for I wish all money to be put to her benefit. If this is unnecessary, the money should be held in trust for my grandchildren.'

Paul Francis had snorted over that. It was unlikely Arthur Egan's estate would amount to very much after the costs of administration and other bills were paid. Looking around the house now, Ward was inclined to agree. But the letter, in Egan's handwriting apparently, but with no superscription and no signature, was an odd way to hand over an administration. It was as though reluctance, or secretiveness, had dogged the old man on his death bed.

Ward sat down at the table, thinking. There was no point in making an inventory this evening – even if he had time. And though it was a typical minion's job, he felt he would be justified in calling in an estate agent; it was reasonable, whatever the heir or heirs might say later. If there were any heirs; nothing was disclosed on the meagre file. No heirs, no money.

No money. And no personal effects at the hospital. A wallet with five pounds in it, but no personal mementoes, it seemed. Odd. Ward rose, and prowled around the kitchen, thinking. Paul Francis obviously hadn't looked closely through Egan's things – one look at the file and he'd discounted it as a valuable estate to administer. But where would an old man keep his personal effects?

The answer was obvious. Ward climbed the stairs, opened the wardrobe, searched through the pockets of the suit, and two changes of clothing hanging there. Nothing, apart from matches, cigarettes, the usual rubbish that a man accumulated in his pockets. Intrigued suddenly, Ward worked swiftly through the drawers of the dressing-table. They were virtually empty.

He sat down on the edge of the bed, frowning. Egan had died of cancer. The hospital seemed to know little about him; notes on the file suggested there were no friends or relatives to be contacted. The hospital had arranged his burial and there had been no mourners.

'Hallooo!'

The voice echoed through the house and Ward rose, went to the top of the stairs. In the cool dimness he could see Mrs Towers from next door peering up at him. 'Wondered if you'd like a cup of tea,' she lied. 'Door was open.'

Ward came down the stairs. 'No, thank you. I'll be leaving in a few minutes. I just called in for a preliminary look around.'

'All have to be sold, won't it?' Mrs Towers said. 'When it is, wouldn't mind first offer of that three-piece in there.'

'I expect it'll go to auction.'

'Ah.' She folded her arms across her narrow bosom, and expressed disappointment. 'Who'll get the money that's left, afterwards?'

'I don't know.' Ward hesitated, then asked, 'Did you know his ... child?'

She stared at him for a moment, then pursed her lips and shook her head. 'Didn't know he had any kids. Never saw them around here if he did. Never saw anyone around here for that matter. Bert used to have a chat with him, occasionally, when he was in the garden. Liked him, Bert did.' She hesitated. 'It's Bert been doin' the garden since Egan's dead. Keepin' up appearances, like. And because Bert liked him.' She shuffled carpet-slippered feet. 'Got some of the old man's tools, by the way. For the gardening.'

'I should think that'll be all right,' Ward said carefully. 'What ... what was Egan like, then?'

'Quiet, kept to himself. No visitors. I remember him movin' in. Years ago now. But he never was very neighbourly. Polite. Kind, in his way. Soft spoken. But kept to himself, if you know what I mean. And ... and there was something else.'

'Yes?'

'He never looked at you. I used to get the feeling that if he passed me in the supermarket he wouldn't recognize me.' She sniffed. 'He did, of course. Always said hello, in fact. But never stopped to chat. Just to Bert, sometimes.'

'What did he do for a living?'

She looked around her, as though measuring the dead man's possessions for signs of accumulated wealth. 'Didn't have a bad job, up until a year before he died. Cancer, wasn't it? Yes... He worked as a market gardener, over Stanley way somewhere. Travelled every day on the bus. Must have saved a bit – no car or nothin', just himself to keep. Still, you can't tell, can you?'

There was a slight challenge in her voice as though she felt Eric Ward could tell. He wasn't prepared to, and when the silence that fell between them lengthened, Mrs Towers shuffled her carpet slippers again. 'Well, if I can't do anything to help ... we couldn't go to the funeral. Bert had a bad chest. Many there?'

'As far as I understand,' Ward said quietly, 'there was no one there.'

Her eyes told him she took it as a criticism. She turned and marched out of the house. Eric Ward stood in the passageway for a few minutes, thinking about the lonely old man dying of cancer; clearing out houses like this was an unpleasant job. Even a different one like this ... with no personal things. Had the dead man *had* any, or had he cleared them out in anticipation of death? A person of his introverted, secretive nature might well have put his own personal house in order, contemplating death. But not everything; he would not have destroyed everything. *Some* things, *really* personal things a man would keep, and keep close to him in his terminal illness.

But if not in hospital... Eric Ward turned and walked back up the stairs, entered the bedroom and got down on his knees. A moment later he felt the case under the bed and drew it out. Small, leather, the kind of case that might have held Masonic regalia. It was not locked. He sprung open the catches. There were very few items in the case, but they would have been all that remained of the memories of Arthur Egan. A leather wallet, seamed and broken, with the initials A. E. lettered faintly in gold. A sealed envelope. A small folder containing a single page letter and a sheaf of five or six photographs. And a bank book.

The initial deposit had been made in April 1965. No drawings had been made, but the interest had been added, year by year for fifteen years. Ward stared in surprise at the sum stated on the first page of the book. It was written in a neat, front-counter clerk hand. It was for twenty thousand pounds.

'How much?' Paul Francis raised his eyebrows in astonishment. 'Twenty thousand? Where the hell did he get that much from, the secretive old bugger!'

'Life savings, maybe.'

'And the house, too, that'll fetch a bit. What do you reckon?'

Ward shrugged. 'About fifteen thousand, maybe. He had a mortgage on it – there's some five thousand outstanding. He must have taken an extension of the mortgage at some time, to still owe that much after fifteen years with inflation the way it's been. Anyway, it comes to a reasonable sum for distribution – say thirty thousand.'

'Let me see the letter again.' Francis took it and read it aloud. 'Well, we'll have to try to find this kid of his, I suppose. Not that he'll deserve the money, if you ask me. I gather the old man lived alone, never got visitors.'

'Who never received visitors?' the voice came from the open doorway.

Ward swung around. Joseph Francis, the senior partner in Francis, Shaw and Elder stood in the doorway, a file in his hand.

Paul Francis stood up, shuffling his papers. 'We were talking about this administration file, sir. On Arthur Egan. Seems he lived alone. But the estate should come to some thirty thousand.'

'Is that so?' Joseph Francis said flatly, uninterested in what his son was saying. 'I gather you'll be helping us with the Morcomb matter, Eric. Had time to have a look at it yet?'

'Not in any detail. I thought at the weekend...'

'Yes. Long-running business. Anyway–'

'Something puzzles me,' Ward said sud-

29

denly, as the senior partner began to turn away.

'About the Morcomb file?'

'No. About this Arthur Egan business.'

'Yes?' Joseph Francis had a narrow, patrician face; his silver hair was always neatly parted, smoothed back, never out of place. It was like his face: Ward felt that each morning Joseph Francis arranged his features and kept them that way, unruffled, unmoved, imperturbable. And his voice was similarly controlled – smoothly modulated, a hint of boredom, an affectation that in an odd way served to accentuate his efficiency and sharpness of mind. Or maybe the affectation merely left a client with that impression – behind the cool, casual manner hummed a sound legal brain. But however a man could order his face and his voice and his manner, there was one thing, in Ward's experience, he could not completely control. His eyes. And for one brief moment Joseph Francis had allowed something to flicker through his old, uninterested glance.

'I'm just puzzled as to why Egan should have nominated us in the way he did.'

There was a short silence. Joseph Francis stared at him, but his eyes seemed to look beyond him, searching the past.

'Maybe ... maybe he'd just heard about us in the town,' Paul Francis offered.

Joseph Francis flickered a quick glance at his son, then gave a little shake of his head. 'No, I imagine it will have been because we once acted for him.'

'He was an old client of ours?' Paul said. 'Ah well, that explains it.'

Not for Eric Ward. 'It was an odd way to ask us to take on the administration, even so,' he said.

Joseph Francis regarded him for a few moments. 'Perhaps the letter ... I admit it was an odd way to give us the work ... perhaps it was something he was hesitating over. A reluctance...'

Ward waited a moment, but the senior partner seemed suddenly lost in thought. 'Reluctance to face up to the fact he was dying?'

A faint smile touched Joseph Francis's cold lips. 'I think not. More probably, a reluctance to be reminded of the past.'

He turned to go, again, but Eric Ward persisted. 'When he was a client of the firm, you mean?'

Joseph Francis looked back over his shoulder. He hesitated, then nodded. 'Yes, I would think so. And in a way it's rather flattering that he nominated us. I can't say we – we did very much for him at the time.'

Arthur Egan. The words stirred in Eric Ward's brain. There was something... 'What did he ask the firm to do for him, then?'

But it had slipped into place for him even before Joseph Francis answered.

'He asked us to arrange his defence to a charge of murder.'

4

Eric Ward took the Morcomb file home to Wylam at the weekend and spent most of Friday evening reading it. After supper he took a walk along the river bank; the moon was high, the dark water gleaming beyond the bridge. To walk like this eased him after a hard day's work and, he hoped, it eased the tension that might bring him another painful attack. In the sky the orange glow that was the lights of Newcastle extended in a long arc until it faded against the pearl-string of lights rising up towards Stanley. It was up there somewhere that Arthur Egan had worked as a market gardener.

Arthur Egan.

He *had* known the name, if not the man.

Eric Ward had been a young policeman, not involved in the case itself, but hearing a certain amount about it as it had proceeded. Robbery, burglary, and a struggle with an armed householder. The charge had been murder, but at the end of the trial a conviction for manslaughter had been brought in. It still gave Arthur Egan a stiff prison sentence, Ward seemed to recall as Joseph Francis had remarked, the solicitors had not done a great deal for him in their briefing of the defending counsel; even so, Egan had remembered the firm and asked them, in his curious, secretive manner, to administer his estate.

As he walked along the river bank Ward could hear the soft chuckling of the water, an occasional splash as a nocturnal animal entered the stream under the alder bushes that flanked its edge, but he was hardly aware of his surroundings. He was thinking about the house in Westerhope, with its evidence of a quiet restrained lifestyle. Arthur Egan had left prison and found a job as a market gardener and then, effectively, dropped out of the public eye. And, it would seem, the eye of his family. No son had come to the funeral; no relative. And the letter to Francis, Shaw and Elder had been reluctant: the man had not enjoyed opening up the link with his past.

He had tried to make a new life for himself, and succeeded, until the end.

As Eric Ward hoped to succeed... He still had doubts. They came, at their blackest, when the pain ripped at him late at night, when he looked back at a career in the Force that had achieved little, at a marriage that had broken down after five years when his lonely wife had sought solace elsewhere, and at a growing physical disability that struck at the very root of his pride. He liked what he was doing; he might have turned to legal practice in any case. But the *choice* had not been his and when the doubts came he locked himself away like this, alone on a river bank, as enclosed by the evening silence as he would be by any darkened room.

On the Saturday morning Ward drove into town early, did enough shopping to see him through the week, and after a coffee in the Eldon Centre, retrieved his car to drive back to Wylam. He took a light lunch; then settled down again to the Morcomb file, to familiarize himself with the main issues involved in the case and obtain some understanding of the background. It was a complicated enough matter to engross him throughout the afternoon: a decision had been taken by the Lands Tribunal against which Lord

Morcomb had appealed; the appeal had been heard by the Court of Appeal, who had made an order rejecting the application and supporting the decision of the Lands Tribunal; now, Lord Morcomb, who seemed to be a rather determined individual, was pressing for a further – and final – appeal to the House of Lords; not that Eric Ward criticized him for that, when the matter involved an estate worth in excess of three million pounds.

By five o'clock he had had enough. He took a bath and as he lay in the hot water his thoughts returned again to Arthur Egan. He had brought the Egan file home with him in the car but he had not yet looked closely at the contents of the dead man's wallet. He had been somewhat reluctant to do so: Arthur Egan had been a near recluse in terms of his personal life and it seemed wrong now to pry into those possessions that he had deemed the only ones worth keeping.

It had to be done, nevertheless, and after he had dressed he went down to the small front room he used as an office and opened the briefcase containing the Egan file.

He spread the few relics of Arthur Egan's life in front of him. The seamed leather wallet; the single-page letter; the photographs, and the sealed envelope.

He had not opened the envelope; he had felt it with his fingers and guessed it held very little, and not a sheet of paper, but now, gently, he teased open the flap. The light gum had lost its adhesiveness and it came away quickly. He looked inside the envelope but did not remove its contents.

There was just a thick lock of blond hair.

Eric Ward sat staring at the lock for a little while. It could have been Egan's sentimental remembrance of his child, or of a lost love, or of his mother. Ward suspected he would never discover which, now the colour of a person's hair changed as much as his appearance and character changed, over the years.

He turned to the photographs. There were six of them. One was of a young man of perhaps sixteen years of age: a bright, smiling face, a boyish lock of hair falling in his eyes; a grin that would win him friends. He was looking into the sun and though it robbed his face of character, there was yet enough in the snapshot to suggest that the boy had a liveliness of spirit that would make men like him and women love him. There was a second snapshot of the same person, taken perhaps five years earlier, and a third, of a

36

man with his arms linked with the boy. Eric Ward set them aside; they would do to begin enquiries.

He picked up the other three. One was of a baby, but there was no way of telling when the photograph had been taken, nor of the sex of the child. Ward stared at it, guessing it could well be the child who would be heir to Egan's thirty thousand. The next two photographs were a surprise. The first one was of a churchyard, with cypress in the background and part of a Norman tower at the left, but it was blurred and difficult to make out. The last snapshot had probably been taken in the same churchyard; it displayed less background and concentrated on a single, unpretentious tombstone. The photographer had been no expert; it was impossible to make out the name or the epitaph on the stone for the angle at which the sunlight struck the stone rendered it unreadable.

That left only the letter; a single page, it told Eric Ward very little.

'Dear Arthur, I've managed to do what I said could be arranged. The job is yours if you want it. I've already phoned the owner and told him to expect you on Tuesday. Take this letter with you and show him. That'll be all that's necessary. So,

watch how you go, lad, and good luck. And no more nonsense, hey? Yours sincerely Fred.'

'It's not much to go on.' Jackie Parton squinted at the photographs and read the letter again, then shrugged his narrow shoulders. 'Doesn't even give me anything to start with.'

Ward smiled, rose, and bought the little man another pint of Brown. As he waited for his change he glanced back to the table where the ex-jockey sat. Jackie Parton had never had much trouble with his weight as a jockey, riding mostly at Newcastle and the northern racetracks at York and Ripon, and it seemed as though his liking for brown ale did little to affect his weight now that he had retired. He looked as lean and weathered as he had during his riding days, and his grey eyes were as sharp as ever. He looked up and caught Ward's glance; he grinned, a cheeky, infectious grin that was now slightly lopsided because of the scar along his lip. 'I think this one could cost you, Eric,' he called.

Ward carried the drink back to the table and set it down carefully. His own lemonade was still half full. He sat down and smiled at Parton. 'How's your luck these days, anyway, Jackie?'

The little man shrugged and reached for his glass. 'Going well enough, considering. I don't make nothing like I made in the good days, of course, but I pick up a bit of training down Harrogate way from time to time and then there's the occasional ... commissions like this.' His glance wandered to the lemonade. 'And how's yours?'

'Let's say I hope to ... survive. You ... er ... you get no work up around this way then, with the horses?'

Jackie Parton scratched his lean cheek, then took a long drink. 'You blow the gaff on a couple of people up here and it's not so easy to make a living afterwards. Oh, I'm not saying the trainers and owners are scared to employ me, or even intimidated, but, well, I guess they consider life is likely to be more peaceful if they have nothing for me.

'But you've still got your contacts?'

'That's why you're employing me.'

They were unrivalled. Jackie Parton was a product of the Scotswood Road who had clawed his way out of the slums to cross the river and, horse-crazy, obtain employment at a stables in Durham. Within two years he had made a reputation for himself as a promising rider and a free spender. By the time he was twenty he was well-known in every club in

Newcastle, Durham County and down to the coast. His circle of acquaintances widened and he visited the clubs and brothels in Byker; he gained his own following at the Newcastle races, not only from the racing fraternity itself, but from a large number of working-class people to whom he became an idol matching those who bestrode the fields at Roker Park and Gallowgate. Then, when he was thirty, a steward's enquiry at York was followed by another at Newcastle and it was said that he had been involved with an illegal betting syndicate. His racing career fell apart, and one night he was found in a back street near Dog Leap Stairs, with broken ribs, a pulped face and a scarred mouth. There were no more offers of rides thereafter – but his friends had not forgotten him.

'Well, you can make a start in one of your old haunts,' Ward suggested. 'I've not yet had time to do much checking, but Arthur Egan hailed from Byker in the first instance, that much I know from the newspaper reports.'

'Newspapers?'

'A murder charge, years ago.'

'Egan ... ahhh.' Parton's eyes narrowed with memory; he also recalled something of the case. 'Yeah, all right, there's people I can see in Byker might give me a lead.' He hesi-

tated. 'There's ... er ... there's nothing dicey about this job, is there, Eric? I need to know; people will ask, and I'll have to tell them straight.'

'No problems, Jackie. It's a simple administration matter. He left some money, and I need to trace his – family to distribute that money. That's all. There'll be ads in all the local newspapers soon, asking for information and so on, inviting the heirs to contact us. It's straight stuff.'

'And these photographs?' Parton asked.

'Take them. Show them around. I don't know who the young lad is, but maybe you can find out. And the baby – could be that's the son we're looking for. Or daughter, whichever it is. As for the letter, you'd better leave it with me. It's possible it was his letter of introduction to the market gardener job, but I can check on that.'

Jackie Parton grimaced. 'And that's all there was, hey?'

'Apart from a lock of blond hair.'

'A *sentimental* killer?'

The words jarred on Eric Ward in a manner that surprised him. He knew that Arthur Egan had been a killer; the law had said so. In fact, that was almost all he did know about the man, and yet having visited his house,

41

and gone through the dead man's possessions, he now felt a certain resentment that Parton should use the word *killer* in referring to Arthur Egan.

The ex-jockey was watching him closely. 'What's the matter, Eric?'

Ward stared at him, not realizing he had allowed his feelings to show in his face. He managed a faint smile. 'I don't know, really. It's just that ... well, Egan's paid whatever debt he owed.'

Parton nodded slowly, his eyes not leaving Ward's face. 'I take the point... Anyway, I'll make a start tonight – I intended going over to the Acorn Club and that's where I make one contact to start with. I ... er ... I don't suppose you'd be wanting to join me?'

Ward shook his head, grimacing at the lemonade. 'I'd likely as not be thrown out.'

Parton laughed. 'They're very understanding in Byker. They'd just think you were a poof.' He stood up, drained his glass. 'I'll be in touch, Eric. See you.'

The little man walked away on bow legs, hands deep in the pockets of his hacking jacket and a couple of men at the bar called out to him as he passed. He stopped briefly to speak to them and left them laughing loudly.

It was Jackie Parton's kind of pub. The lounge bar of an establishment that just hovered on the sleazy side; the kind of city centre house that contained a balance of thuggish young men and prosperous, well dressed middle-aged men of consequence. Few women; sporting talk; a lot of beer drunk; but never any trouble. The young hooligans who brought the patrol cars down in droves to Northumberland Street on a Saturday night stayed away from this hostelry. They were out of their class.

Ward finished his lemonade and rose, glancing around. There was one man sitting alone, a little distance apart from the bar and there was something familiar about the set of his broad shoulders. Ward hesitated, then, recognizing him, decided to leave without greeting him. Just as suddenly, he changed his mind.

He walked across the room and stood in front of the big man with the piggy eyes and belligerent mouth. 'Hello, Dick. It's been a long time.'

The piggy eyes. Flicked an uninterested glance up to him and then looked away again. 'It has. Saw you across the room but you seemed to be having an earnest. Funny company.'

'Jackie Parton's all right. Doing some work for me.'

'Parton, a grass?' The little eyes betrayed a weary surprise. 'Never knew that.'

'You've got it wrong. I'm not with the Force any longer. I'm working with a solicitor, and Jackie's making some enquiries for me.'

'Ah yes, come to think of it, I'd heard.' A certain bitter irony crept into his voice. 'We got that much in common then, hey, Eric? Forced retirement.'

Eric Ward stared at the pudgy features of ex-Detective-Inspector Dick Kenton and wanted to disagree. In his book, there was a great difference between being forced to retire on grounds of ill-health and a retirement made necessary by the kicking of a drunken prisoner almost to death in a night cell in Whitley Bay. But he did not say it. Instead, he offered to buy Kenton a drink. The ex-detective drained his pint glass by way of answer.

When Ward returned with the pint refilled, Kenton raised his eyebrows. 'Not drinking, yourself?'

Ward shook his head. 'Doctor's orders,' he said shortly. 'How are things with you?'

Kenton took a long swallow. 'Bloody. Security Officer at Marshall's. Damn all to do because they won't put out the money to do anything as far as security is concerned. They just rely on the villains knowing I'm around, and at nights too. That's enough to scare off any of the scrubbers around here, you reckon?'

Ward managed a grin and nodded. He could understand the viewpoint – if Kenton ever did catch anyone breaking and entering at Marshall's the matter would hardly be referred to the police authorities. 'And you,' Kenton was saying. 'You've gone and joined the bloody enemy. But then, you always was an intellectual bastard. While I sweated my inspector's exams you sailed on to take a law course at the poly. No substitute, you know; no substitute for the beat, and the chat in the clubs and the hard graft.'

'I know it.'

'That's how I came to grief, you know. Made too many enemies – and old Ironguts Starling didn't have the courage to back me up when I was only ... ah, the hell with it. So what you working on at the moment, then? Affiliation proceedings?'

Ward ignored the sneer. He hesitated. 'Just an administration matter. Chap called Egan's just died. You might remember him. I seem to recall you were on the investigating team at the time.'

Kenton repeated the name to himself, several times, then lolled back in his chair. He had been away from the Force for four years now, and the period had bloated his body, fleshed out his face, made his eyes seem piggier than ever, but they had not affected his card-index mind, and he was thinking back now, not because he had difficulty recalling the name but simply because he wanted to bring back all the important details. 'Egan ... yeah, I got him now. Dead, is he? Huh. Haven't heard of him in years.'

'He dropped out of sight, virtually. Took a job. Lived quietly.'

'I reckon.' Kenton nodded, as though something was being confirmed for him. 'He was never your usual kind of villain. In fact...'

As Kenton paused, thinking, Ward asked, 'How exactly did the charge arise, Dick?'

Kenton remained silent for almost a minute as, with his eyes half closed, he went back over the case in his mind. Then he looked at Ward, who was surprised to see the resentment in the man's glance. 'Starling was a bastard, wasn't he?' When Eric made no reply, Kenton went on, 'He railroaded me, you know. That little sod from Whitley Bay, he was my fixer on a factory job at Team Valley,

46

but he ran out on me. I got him down at the Bay, and the lads gave me the use of a cell. Hell, we all did it, and still do! But he was scared, the little bugger, and I had to put the arm on him.' He paused, reviewing old injustices, and he shook his heavy head. 'All right, maybe I went too far, but you expect your Chief to cover. He had done in the past, when it suited him. Not this time: he was near retirement, wasn't he? So I got the chop. And I'm a security officer at Marshall's when I could have been a super in a cosy office job. Starling ... you know what he's doing? Farming. Bloody farming, up Jedburgh way.'

Ward was puzzled. Kenton grinned maliciously. 'Starling was a Chief Superintendent in those days, when Egan got put away. Didn't remember that, did you? Need a memory like mine, for that.'

'Starling was in charge of the investigation?' Ward asked.

'Right. And I was dogs bodying, along with a lad called ... wait a minute ... Arkwright ... Yorkshire lad, right twit. It was him that found the clincher.'

'Against Egan?'

'Right. Well, one of the clinchers, anyway. There were others, and it was a pretty tight case.'

'Reduced to manslaughter.'

'Way of the world and our revered judges. You don't remember much about it, do you, Eric? Well, as I recall, it would have been a straight enough burglary in the first instance. Colonel ... Colonel Denby, some manor house up in Northumberland. Trouble was, you know what these damned retired colonels are like. Still think they're in the bloody army. Egan broke in, got disturbed and ran for it. Denby ended up getting shot. Robbery with violence, burglary, murder. But seems the shotgun was Denby's, he had already fired one shot, and when he was prepared to let Egan have the other right in his face, Egan clubbed him with a handy iron stanchion from the bridge they were standing on. Self-defence, his lawyers claimed. The jury said manslaughter. And he got ... ten years?'

'He did seven.'

Kenton shrugged indifferently. He sipped his beer, thoughtfully. 'No prints on the bar, of course.'

'So how did they catch Egan?'

'Egan walked away, leaving Denby dying. He was carrying some jewellery and silver ornaments. Stupid fool tried to fence them with Tiggy Williams. One of the first places

48

we tried. Picked up some pieces and Tiggy hauled him out of a line-up.'

Ward frowned. 'Did Egan have a previous record, then?'

'You mean how come he was put in the line-up in the first place? Ah well, no previous record, but other evidence linking him with the crime. To start with, as I recall, they used dogs which pointed them towards Egan's place. A cottage, not too far from Denby's residence. And then there was the clothing Egan burned – there was some woman who came up with evidence of that.'

'His wife?'

'Wife?' Kenton bared his teeth in a thoughtful grimace. 'Lived alone, as I remember. Didn't have a wife on the premises. No, this biddy was, I don't know, dairymaid or something, working around the stables, something like that. It's what Egan was doing I believe. Anyway, she shopped him – though we couldn't get much from it. I mean, forensic sifted the furnace he used and got buttons and such like, but only her word it was bloodstained clothing. The jury believed her, anyway. She was a good witness. Positive, like.' He hesitated again, staring at his beer. 'They was all so positive, in fact.'

'But that was the case?'

49

Kenton nodded. 'Apart from Arkwright's clincher. Don't get me wrong. Egan was guilty. He pulverised that old bastard all right. I mean, he never even raised anything other than self-defence at the trial. Say that for him; he took his medicine. But Starling: I should have known even then what a bastard he was. You know, Eric, whatever I did in the Force I always played fair. I used my muscle, I put in the boot, but only when I knew I was dealing with a villain. And I always played fair, didn't I?'

There was a maudlin appeal in the man's little eyes.

Ward had no liking for Kenton and had always detested his methods but he knew what Kenton meant, and he was forced to agree. Kenton had been a rough, aggressive and brutal enforcer of what he saw as the law – but he had never been described as anything other than straight. He nodded. 'I've never heard otherwise, Dick.'

'Well, that wasn't Starling's way,' Kenton said bitterly. 'And I should have been more careful when I was down at Whitley Bay that night. I should have known Starling wouldn't back me when it came to it. He was always a main chancer – I knew that from the Egan case, anyway.'

50

Ward leaned forward. 'What do you mean?'

'Hell's flames, you know how these things work as well as I do! Look, the dogs pointed us towards the stables and Egan's cottage. It wasn't easy, there'd been rain, and it took us several days, but we managed to pull out the story of the burned clothing, and then we got the lucky bit from Tiggy Williams, so we pulled Egan in to face him. But even that might not have been enough. So Starling sent us out to do a second search of Egan's cottage. And Arkwright came up with the clincher.'

'Which was?'

'A silver brooch. Hidden in the drainpipe outside the cottage. It was identified as belonging to Colonel Denby's wife. So there we were. Burned clothing. Possession of stolen articles. Identification from a fence. Starling had his case.'

Ward had an idea what Kenton was trying to say. 'Spell it out, Dick,' he said quietly.

'This was a *second* search, my friend. We'd gone over that cottage with a fine-tooth comb because we were *certain*, from Starling down, that Egan had hammered old Denby. And we had some pretty good evidence against him. But we needed a clincher. And – happy days – there it was after Starling sent us in again. Thing was,' Kenton scowled, 'I searched that bloody drainpipe on the first time round. And there was damn all in there the first time!'

'Egan could have put it in there between the two searches,' Ward suggested.

Kenton's contemptuous glance told Ward what he thought of that theory. 'I was assigned a different part of the cottage. Starling was there personally for the second search. He sent that twit Arkwright to search outside. And when I said there had been nothing there first time we looked Starling called me an incompetent bastard, and did I know that I could have cost them Egan's head? The way he spoke, you'd have thought it was his head on the block.'

And perhaps Chief Superintendent Starling had seen it that way: on the promotional block, at least. As he lay in bed that night, thinking back over his conversation with Dick Kenton, Eric Ward considered the career of James Starling. A rapid rise in the Northumberland force, then from Chief Superintendent he had moved south, to an Assistant Chief Constable post; a second move to hold a Deputy's job for five years had led to a triumphant return, eventually, to become Chief Constable with the force in which he had started his career.

And now he was farming near Jedburgh.

It was easy to allow resentment to colour judgement. He himself, now the Force was behind him, could feel anger at that Force simply because his incapacitating illness had rendered him useless in their eyes. With Kenton it was worse. He had been drummed out for brutality, for doing something he had, essentially, believed in. That kind of experience could jaundice a man's vision, sharpen his resentments to such a pitch that, in a dead-end job outside, he would be prepared to malign his superior officers. Not just prepared ... he would feel the need to do so, until trivial incidents were magnified out of proportion and accusations made against honourable men.

Arthur Egan had killed Colonel Denby. All the evidence had pointed to it, and Egan had himself accepted his punishment quietly and uncomplainingly. There had been no appeal against sentence, it seemed. Whether Kenton was right or wrong about Starling's planting of evidence, it made no difference either way. Egan had been guilty; he had served his term of imprisonment.

And now he was dead.

And Eric Ward's task was to discover the whereabouts of Egan's heir, not to wonder about the commission of a twenty-year old crime.

Chapter Two

1

Nevertheless, during the course of the following week Eric Ward found his thoughts constantly returning to the conversation with Kenton. He had plenty of work to occupy his time and his mind but the Egan file hovered constantly on the fringes of his consciousness. He arranged for advertisements to be placed in the north-eastern newspapers, calling for any relatives of Arthur Egan, deceased, to make contact with Francis, Shaw and Elder, and he did some more work on the Morcomb case, briefing Paul in one long session on the Wednesday afternoon.

Paul Francis seemed particularly difficult that afternoon. He had been to a Law Society party the previous evening and had not recovered from his hangover all day. As

Eric discussed the Morcomb file with him, he obtained the impression that the young solicitor hardly heard him and it was with a gesture of impatience that Paul finally brought the conversation to a halt.

'Look, it's perfectly obvious to me that you've had time to go into the file in some detail. I haven't; I've just been too damn busy. The best thing will be for you to be present when we meet Lord Morcomb; Joe will be boning up on the file and you can fill in details on the action itself. I'll just concentrate on the early background and that way we can present a united front and help each other out.'

Ward stared at him. If Joseph Francis could have heard the manner in which his son was dismissing such an important matter as the Morcomb case he would have gone white with anger, losing his much vaunted controlled indifference. Ward kept his own temper; he was just the lackey. 'If that's the way you want it, Paul.'

Francis was aware of the veiled contempt in Ward's tone and it did nothing to mollify his bad humour. 'You taken out letters of administration on the Egan estate yet?'

'The application is in.'

'What about the assets themselves?'

'I've engaged an estate agent to make a professional valuation of the house and I've been in touch with the bank holding the money to explain the position to them. They'll release the money as soon as the necessary searches have been completed and the beneficiaries to Egan's estate located.'

Paul scowled; his head was throbbing still. 'You managed to trace any relative yet?'

'Not yet. I've got someone working on it.'

'Who?'

'Jackie Parton.'

'Oh God, that little runt. What's wrong with the detective agency we usually use?'

Ward shrugged. 'I thought with a case like this – I mean, all we know is that Egan came from Byker – it might be more sensible to use someone with strong local connections.'

'Ah, well, you may be right. Anyway, I've arranged with my secretary for you to deal with a couple more conveyances that have been hanging fire on my desk. They'll come through this afternoon. Anything else?'

Ward hesitated. 'I just wondered whether the Egan file would still be here in the office.'

Paul Francis stared at him, uncomprehending, for a few moments. 'You mean the old file, when we acted for him on the murder charge? I wouldn't know, but if it is it'll be upstairs in the attic by now.' He paused, eyeing Eric carefully. 'But you don't want to go wasting time on old stuff like that.'

Eric agreed and left the room. Within the hour the two conveyances arrived and he spent a couple of hours on them. It was gone five o'clock when he had finished and his eyelids were puffy. He sensed that another attack might be coming so he went to the washroom, anticipating trouble this time, and applied some of his eye-drops. Back in his office, he put his head back on the chair and closed his eyes, waiting for the drops to take effect.

Faded photographs flashed before his mind. A man, a boy, a child, a graveyard. Sad, unexplained remnants of a man's life. A slim file from which to discover a man's secrets.

But there might be something in the other file.

It was five-thirty when Eric climbed the stairs to the attic rooms. The offices of Francis, Shaw and Elder were situated in a large, three-storied house in Gosforth, with reception rooms on the ground floor, and partners' offices above the typists, on the first and second floors. A small law library took up the largest room on the second floor and at the end of the library a narrow wooden staircase gave access to the attic rooms. The filing system used by the firm could hardly be described as efficient in business terms but it sufficed, and old files were retained upstairs, out of the way, gathering dust.

As soon as Ward entered the attic he realized there was little chance of his finding the old Egan file. Whereas below the files were kept in cabinets, here many of them had been stacked on the floor, with little regard, as far as he could make out, for logical sequence. Some seemed to be stacked alphabetically; others in an arithmetic sequence he did not understand; yet others piled according to the year on the cover. Some of them went back to 1898.

'We're quite an old firm, my boy,' said the quiet voice from the doorway.

Ward started guiltily. He swung around, his hands dusty, his clothing stained, to see Joseph Francis standing in the doorway, a quizzical smile on his face. 'It's unusual to see articled clerks working at six-thirty, particularly up here. What are you looking for? Maybe I can help.'

Six-thirty. Involuntarily, Ward glanced at his watch.

He hadn't realized he'd been here so long.

Francis must have heard him moving about above, and come up to investigate. 'I ... I've been dealing with the Egan administration. I wondered whether there might be anything of use to us to trace his relatives on the old file ... the file when we represented him previously.'

Joseph Francis wrinkled his patrician nose and sniffed. 'It's over twenty years ago, Eric. And I wouldn't even be sure we'd kept the file. Civil matters, estates, trusts, these we keep. Criminal matters ... hardly likely. You're welcome to look, of course, but ah ... it would be a long task, and, I suspect, at the end unrewarding.' He hesitated. 'Since I gather you'll be coming in with us on the Morcomb discussions you'd be better employed knowing that file by heart. And now, it's getting late.' He half turned, paused, and then said, 'Come down to my room and have a sherry.'

There was just enough of a command in the suggestion to make Ward comply. He turned off the lights and followed the senior partner downstairs, pausing only to wash his hands before he joined Francis in his room. It was the largest of the partners' rooms, containing its own law library, books shining in elegant bindings, and with a window overlooking the distant Town Moor.

'Dry or medium?' Francis asked, gesturing towards two cut glass decanters. 'I take it your doctor does allow you to drink?'

'In moderation, sir.' Ward took a glass of medium sherry and Francis toasted his health. The old man then took a seat behind the desk and gestured Ward to a leather armchair, before asking him about his state of health, and whether he enjoyed working for the firm, and how great were the changes he saw between life in the Force and life in the office. Ward gained the impression the old man hardly listened to his answers; there was something else on his mind. At last, abruptly, he asked, 'How do you get on with Paul?'

'Well enough.'

'He works you hard?'

'I think so.'

'Too hard?' Joseph Francis's glance was perceptive. 'Too hard by comparison with his own work rate?'

'I'm in no position to make that kind of judgement, sir.'

'Humph ... I'll be frank, Eric...' But he thought better of it. If he was about to make any criticisms of his son to an articled clerk, he changed his mind. He was a man who rarely failed to control his conversations, and the momentary aberration confused him. In an attempt to reach even ground again, he said, 'This Egan thing. What did you expect to find in an old file?'

'I don't know. Names, dates, places.'

'Connected with the murder, you mean?'

Ward hesitated. 'No, not exactly. Just something that might make the search for the beneficiaries of the estate easier.'

'If you want my opinion, it'll go to the Crown as *bona vacantia*,' Francis spoke indifferently.

'Egan's letter spoke of a child, and grand-children—'

'They could have been figments of his imagination,' Francis said, but then he paused and was lost in thought for several seconds. Ward waited, and at last the old man flicked a quick glance in his direction. 'I've no idea now what might have been on that file, but I recall nothing mentioning family. None came to the trial, you know.'

'He was completely alone?'

'That was the way he wanted it.' Francis hesitated, toying with his sherry glass. 'A strange man, you know. I felt I never got to know him really. In a professional or personal way. He remained ... aloof, indifferent to his fate. He ... well, I told you we did little for him. That was not entirely our own fault. He

61

did little to help himself. We pleaded self-defence after discussions with him, and the facts of the struggle on the bridge came to light—'

'How do you mean?' Ward interrupted.

'There'd been witnesses to the struggle, though they couldn't identify Egan. A courting couple down among the trees; trespassing, of course. After Egan's arrest they came forward, but a long time after. We had to hurry to concoct his defence. Until then we had nothing to go on; he'd not told us that Colonel Denby had levelled the gun at him. I said indifferent to his fate, but somehow that isn't the right word. After all these years, I can't quite recall, but at the time I think I felt he was ... I don't know. Maybe he was a religious man, and wanted to atone for his sins. That was his way.'

'What kind of man was he?' Ward asked.

Joseph Francis sipped his sherry. 'Quiet. Reserved. But obviously hot-tempered – beating Denby the way he did. People can be like that. Well-set man; not exactly a handsome man, but he'd a face you'd remember. A woman would, anyway.'

'Was he guilty of killing Colonel Denby?'

The senior partner stared at Eric Ward in astonishment. 'Good Lord, what do you mean? The evidence was clear, the jury convinced. He was guilty all right but I had the odd feeling that ... well, he didn't feel weighed down by the burden of guilt and yet he wanted to face the penalty for his actions. Strange man.' He finished his sherry. 'Now then, young man, home to Wylam. You'll find out nothing more about the Egan business tonight. Or ever, in my opinion. You'll be lucky to come across any connection of his, if you ask me.'

Ward wondered if Jackie Parton was having any better luck.

She was eighty, dark-shawled, huddled over a coal fire with her boots on the fender, but she still liked what she called her 'bottle o' Broon'. Above and beyond the terrace in which she lived the Byker Wall soared, bright coloured, built to keep out the clamour of a motorway that was never constructed, and changed in concept to become a warren of homes for the dispossessed of the crumbling terraces below. Most of the terraces had gone now, and open, raw tracks of earth awaited development, but she still clung to the old home and the old ways, an open coal fire, a kettle on the hob, and a bottle of brown ale for her supper.

Jackie Parton sat in the wooden-armed chair beside her as she waved her glass in one hand and the half-empty bottle in the other and talked of the days she had left behind her. They were anecdotes of people long since dead, names unknown to him, and he had half forgotten the questions that had prompted them. Uncles, cousins, grandfathers, mothers, they had all come out in a welter of storied incident, mingled with births, deaths and street names.

'Oh, aye, hinny, his mither, I tell ye, she wor a reet hoor!'

Granny Skipton lapsed into a sudden silence, and Jackie Parton leaned forward. 'Whose mother, old lady?'

'The feller you was askin' after. Arthur Egan ... hey, now, he was a bonny lad.'

'And this is him, in the picture here?'

She nodded as he showed her the photograph again; this was as far as he had got half an hour ago. 'Aye, that's him, and he was a bonny lad, a real bonny lad. But his mither ... I tell ye, she was up liftin' her skirts away Scotswood with her man, I was just a wee lass mysel', then, but I remember it clear. She did away to Byker, chasin' after first one man t' other, all the while draggin' her bairn with her. He was a bonny lad, that

Arthur, and good wi' it.'

'Good?'

'Didn't he look after the little one when he came along?' Her voice, querulous, had now taken on a tone of indignation. She waved the bottle in Jackie's face. 'That hoor of a mither of his, she was oot most nights, on the toon, aroun' wi' the men, and she was leavin' Arthur to look after the little one. Aye, he wor a good lad, wor Arthur.'

'This little one you're talking about, Gran.' Jackie thrust the photograph under her nose again. 'Would this be him, in the picture with Arthur?'

'Likely. Can't be certain; moved away, to Henessey Street when I was growed. Looks like him, though, with Arthur. He was a bonny lad, too. A way with the lasses, I heard.'

Jackie Parton stared at the photograph of the young boy with Egan. 'What happened to him?'

'Young Tommy? Went for a seaman, when he was growed.' She began to croon to herself, rocking slightly in the chair, grinning into the glowing coals of the fire. 'And what about Arthur?' He had to repeat the question before she stopped her little song.

'Arthur? Don't know too well. Ye see,

when Tommy was aboot sixteen, that hoor, she went and married again, damned fool he was to have her, and Arthur went away then. Got a job Hexham way, they said. He came back a few times, to see how Tommy was gettin' on; few times, he took Tommy back with him for a few days, but that lad didn't like the country air. After Tommy left to go to sea, didn't see Arthur again, in Byker.'

'Did you ever hear that Arthur got wed?'

'Didn't hear so.'

'While he was around here did he have a ... a lass?' Granny Skipton grinned at him, three blackened teeth in a gaping mouth. 'Had a go at him mesel' once, ye know. Older than him I was, and been around a bit, but he wouldn't have me. Bonny lad, though. A lass? No. Kep' himsel' to himsel', as I recall. Up in Northumberland, now, might have been different. Don't know that.'

'So he didn't have any children by a local girl around Byker?'

Granny Skipton hooted, then threw her greasy apron over her head with her fore-arms, still clutching bottle and glass in her hands. She cackled under the apron for almost a minute before she re-emerged, still grinning. 'Arthur never got anyone in the family way aroun' here – if he had, we'd have knowed all about it.'

Jackie believed it. He hesitated, watching her for a moment. Then, quietly, he said, 'He's dead now, Granny.'

She was unmoved. 'Comes to us all, hinny.'

Jackie still watched her carefully. 'Did you hear about ... about Arthur's trouble with the police, years back?'

She grinned again, but it was a sly, conspiratorial grimace, the closing of minds in a closed area. 'Naw, nivver heard of anything like that aboot Arthur, did we?' Her attention was caught by a bold cockroach making its way across the fender for the shadows of the table leg. She lifted her foot, brought it down deliberately and slowly on the insect and a whitish yellow pus squirted from beneath the sole of her boot. She stared at it stoically. 'Naw. Don't ever know aboot trouble with the polis around here.'

2

Eric Ward received a telephone call at the office from Jackie Parton next morning. The ex-jockey explained that he had spent his time – and the firm's money – to some effect at least. Enquiries at the clubs had sent him to several streets in the Byker area and eventually he had met an old lady called Skipton who remembered the family well enough. He explained that Arthur Egan's father would seem to have died when Arthur was quite young and that his mother had looked to other men for support. One of them had fathered a child on her, then deserted her; Arthur had helped bring up the boy, Tommy, until a seaman called Andrews had married Arthur's mother. Arthur had then left.

'Where did he go then?'

'It seems he went to work at some stables or other in Northumberland. Granny Skipton said Hexham way, but others say not. There was a farm mentioned in the reports ... and if it's not far from Colonel Denby's manor house, it can hardly be Hexham way. I'll check, anyway.'

'The boy in the picture?'

'That's Tommy ... Tommy Andrews. He took his stepfather's name. And followed in his steps. Went off to sea; not been heard of since, not Byker way, at least.'

'Hmmm. I got in touch with London, by the way, and got a search done for Arthur Egan's marriage. There wasn't one. Nothing recorded.'

'No local lasses either,' Parton reported. 'So the plot thickens. I suppose the answer is we'll have to see if he laid any of the dairy-maids around the local farms in Northumberland now. That'll be a long job, if you ask me.'

'There's money to back it ... for a while.' The law required Eric Ward to make all reasonable enquiries before the estate could be regarded as *bona vacantia,* but the question was, where did reasonable enquiries end? 'Anyway, a few trips out in the country will do you no harm and you might come up with something. Keep in touch.'

'I'll do that – but something on account would help.'

Eric Ward laughed. 'I'll arrange something for you in a couple of days. Against itemized expenses.'

'Including a bottle of "broon"?'

The trouble was, of course, the trail was so cold. Arthur Egan had died of cancer at the relatively young age of fifty-five. He had spent some fifteen years after his release from prison working in Stanley and living a quiet, unobserved life. The seven years prior to that had been spent in prison, and people forgot during that span of time. He would have left Byker perhaps in his early twenties, over thirty years ago, and it would be difficult now to trace people who might remember whether or not Arthur Egan had got a young girl in trouble.

For he had certainly not been married.

Eric Ward wondered about that. There was the possibility that this was nothing but a wild goose chase. The Arthur Egan who had died in Westerhope would have been a different person from the young man who lived in Byker. And Ward knew how life in prison could change a man. It seemed to have made Egan shun society and live a lonely, enclosed life. Perhaps that very loneliness had eventually closed in on him until he had begun to people it with persons of his own imaginings, family who had never existed.

A child who had never been born.

The letter from the Egan file lay on his desk. Ward picked up the phone and dialled the number of the market garden in Stanley where Arthur Egan had worked for almost fifteen years.

Yes, of course they remembered Arthur Egan; very well, in fact. Been with them a long time, he had. No, couldn't remember when he'd started, but it would be when Bob Jackson was running the place. Bob? He was dead, now: bronchial pneumonia six years ago. No, there was no one around who'd be able to say who might have put Arthur Egan in the way of a job at Stanley.

Eric Ward put down the phone. Another dead end.

Testily, he put the letter back in the file and pushed it to one side. He was spending too much time, too much thought on the estate of Arthur Egan. He couldn't account for what seemed to be developing into an obsession with him. From the glance that Paul Francis cast in his direction, when he came into the room five minutes later and saw the file on his desk, he knew that the young solicitor was of the same opinion.

'Aren't you ready, for God's sake? You know we're expected at Lord Morcomb's place. Look, I'll take Joe; you'd better come along in your own car. It'll save me coming back to the office, anyway. But get a move on. We mustn't keep his lordship waiting!'

Eric enjoyed the drive out to the Morcomb estates. The road took him off the main road north beyond Scots Gap and he was skirting wooded hills and rolling fells, dipping past craggy outcrops of rock and tiny farms nestling in little valleys until the sweep of the moorland opened out before him and he could see the crest of Carter Bar beyond Jedburgh, barring the entrance to Scotland. Swinging left, the road was quiet, winding along beside the river, dropping down into a long valley where, according to Paul Francis's instructions, Lord Morcomb now lived, at Sedleigh Hall.

When he entered the narrow roadway pheasant strutted across his path, forcing him to slow, and magpies planed across the fields to his right. On his left the trees were dense, but he caught a glimpse of an ornamental lake encrusted with water-lilies and on a promontory a bell-topped tower, a crumbling folly half hidden by silver birch. Then the roadway opened out ahead of him: the entrance to the courtyard was dominated by a clock tower and when he drove through the archway he found himself beside a green, scattered with small cottages, almost a village in itself. Beyond, on a slight rise, was Sedleigh Hall, Doric-pillared, massive, square-built with wide stone steps, ivy-wreathed walls and high, dominant windows. The late morning sun glinted and flashed on the windows as he drove slowly towards the house; to the left the lawns were bright green and close-cut; to the right a meadow sloped down to the edge of the wood. Beyond, the ground rose again, scarred by an old quarry, evidence that Lord Morcomb's forebears had been prepared to sacrifice view for profit at some time or another, and past the hill, he guessed, would lie the small village of Sedleigh, razed a hundred and fifty years ago to satisfy the lady of the manor's passion for geometric layouts.

He stopped, got out of the car and looked about him.

It was a world away from Newcastle, a million miles from the huddled, ranked terraces of Tyneside, and it gave him the feeling that it would last forever.

Unless the Inland Revenue Commissioners had their way. Paul Francis's car was already there. Eric walked past it and climbed the steps to find that elderly butlers were still in service in some households of consequence; this one opened the door before he rang and when he entered the wide hallway, and stood feeling lost in front of the sweeping oak staircase, a discreet cough turned him towards the library, where he found Joseph Francis and his son waiting with a tall slim young man dispensing glasses of whisky.

Joseph Francis made the introductions. 'Eric Ward – David Penrose. Mr ... ah ...

Penrose acts as Lord Morcomb's estate manager, and is obviously concerned with issues arising out of our visit.'

Joseph appeared slightly uncomfortable. Ward guessed that the senior partner regarded himself as a man of some consequence in the city and was ill at ease here because he felt the pressure of inferiority. It was not so much Penrose's easy manner, as the impending arrival of Lord Morcomb; there could be no question of his lordship meeting them – he would arrive in his time, to consult his legal advisers.

Ward accepted the whisky and water from Penrose almost without thinking, then, holding it without sipping it, walked across to the shelved books. They gleamed at him, row on row, in faultless bindings, probably untouched from one year to the next.

'You like books?'

David Penrose was standing beside him, legs braced, a whisky glass in his hand, the other arm locked behind his back. He had a vaguely proprietorial air about him which surprised Ward. 'I do,' Eric said, 'though I don't know what I'd do with a library of this kind.'

'They look good, of course,' Penrose said. His voice was pleasantly deep, his accent decidedly aristocratic. 'But I did enough reading when I took my degree at the University of Reading. I vowed then I'd work for the outside life and I'd enjoy it, with books out of the window.' He grinned, infectiously; he had good teeth and bright, humorous eyes, dark-lashed above tanned features. Ward liked him, particularly when he lowered his voice and added, 'The old man should be down shortly. He draws no distinction between professional advisers and tradesmen and thinks both should be put in their place. But he's a good stick in his own way. Drink up, and I'll get you another one.'

Ward declined, explaining one was enough for him, and asked Penrose how long he had been working for Lord Morcomb.

'Oh, ever since I took my degree. About ten years, now. I was lucky, really; there was an old chap called Acton here then, but he was pretty old hat in his methods and parts of the estate were quite run down. Lord Morcomb soon found I knew my way around, even if I was a bit on the young side, and retired Acton about four years ago. He appointed me. Like I said – lucky.'

Not so much luck, Ward thought as Penrose walked back to check on the others' drinks. Ability ... and perhaps an eye for the main chance.

'Ah, gentlemen, you being looked after properly? David, doing your duty?'

The voice husked at them from the doorway and Ward swung around to meet Lord Morcomb. He was perhaps seventy years of age, tall, slightly bowed now with a seamed leathery skin in which pouched blue eyes gleamed, all ice and cold light, as he surveyed his advisers in the library. He was dressed in cavalry twill slacks and an old tweed jacket – perhaps de rigueur for lords in country seats, Ward thought to himself – and gave the impression of a man out of his time clinging to the old traditions. But his mouth was thin-lipped and his jaw determined, and Eric Ward guessed Morcomb would be a man dangerous to cross, even at his advanced years. As he came forward there was a certain unsteadiness about his gait, but his grip was strong enough as he condescended to shake hands with his visitors. 'A brandy for me, David,' he said as he walked towards the windows, glanced briefly out across the meadows and then lowered himself into a leather armchair with his back to the light. 'Sit down, gentlemen, sit down. I've taken the liberty to arrange for

some sandwiches to be brought in later –
don't take lunch meself – dinner suits the
digestion better, but we can carry on with
our conversation as you refresh yourselves.
Good of you to come all this way.' His sharp
glance fixed on Ward, weighing him up for a
few moments. 'Yes, good of you to come.'

The preliminaries were over. Joseph Francis cleared his throat. 'My lord, I think it
would be useful if we were all to refresh our
minds about the litigation in question before
we go too far. The previous Lord Morcomb,
with whom you lived, died in 1970.'

'That's right.'

'At which time you inherited the estate.
The properties in question comprised the
Hardford Estate, and those of Sedleigh,
Chaston and Fengrove. These comprised,
principally, farms and farm buildings, small-
holdings, allotments, gardens, agricultural
land, woodyards, residential properties–'

'Sporting rights, ground rents, licensed
houses, yes, yes,' Lord Morcomb interrupted
somewhat testily.

Joseph Francis, surprisingly in view of his
earlier lack of ease, stood his ground.
'Together with certain leases, of quarries and
of collieries.' He cleared his throat again. 'On
the death of your uncle in 1970 estate duty

became payable, and it became a matter of dispute as to how a proper valuation of the estate might be achieved.'

'Dispute is the right word for it,' Lord Morcomb grumbled.

Joseph Francis nodded, then glanced at his son. 'Perhaps you'd like to take it from there, Paul?'

Paul Francis opened his mouth then glanced across to Eric Ward. 'It might be more useful if Eric...'

Aware of the glare Joseph Francis sent in his son's direction, Eric nevertheless knew that he had to save Paul from his lack of work at the weekend. 'As I understand it, Lord Morcomb, and in discussion with Paul, the Lands Tribunal were called upon to consider your appeal against the system of valuation used by the Inland Revenue Commissioners. They in fact upheld the principles used – namely, that the Hardford Estate should be used for the purposes of valuation. They agreed therefore, with the viewing of that estate as 480 separate units, and a valuation of £800,000.' He checked his figures again, swiftly. 'That meant your total estate holdings would produce a valuation of £3,176,650.'

There was a short silence in the room, as

though Eric Ward had said something obscene. For himself, the enormity of the sum came home to him for the first time; for Lord Morcomb, he suspected, it was the size of the valuation against his contentions that kept him silent.

'My valuation and that of my financial advisers,' Lord Morcomb grated, 'is more in the nature of two and a half million.' He glared around him as though daring them dispute his figures. 'And that's where we're stuck.'

'Not quite,' Joseph Francis said nervously. 'We have the fact that the Court of Appeal have now rejected your submissions, upheld the Lands Tribunal and the Commissioners, and really the question is whether you'd be wise at all to press your claim further.'

The morning wore away as Joseph and Ward went over the figures, and the legal principles involved. Lord Morcomb showed his mind was sharp enough when contemplating his own stance, but when Eric attempted to point out the counter-arguments and the possible outcome, he seemed to resist any suggestion that the arguments would hold water.

David Penrose, surprisingly, stepped into the discussion as they paused for their sandwiches and coffee. 'It seems to me, if you'll forgive a lay interpretation of what's going on, that the whole thing comes down to this. Lord Morcomb is arguing that it is unrealistic to split Hardford into 480 units and assume a sale of each of them at the same time.'

'Damn right,' Morcomb grunted. 'Only purchaser would be an investor or a speculator.'

'And he would have to pay a reduced price to safeguard himself against risks, delays and uncertainties in affecting re-sales. There'd also be the costs of such transactions. Accordingly, the sum of £800,000 should be reduced to take this into account.'

'And then there's the time of death,' Morcomb interrupted. 'Don't forget the time of death.'

'That's right.' Penrose agreed earnestly. 'His lordship argues that it is also unreasonable to assume that the valuation should take place at time of death. Rather, it should be construed to mean a reasonable time after the death.'

'And that would mean our figure of two and a half million is nearer the mark. Bloody commissioners!' Lord Morcomb drained his glass and thumped it down on the table.

Ward was watching Penrose. The estate

manager seemed to have a considerable grasp of the principles involved and it was obvious that Lord Morcomb used him as a confidant, trusting in his abilities. But there were problems in his summary, already dealt with by the Court of Appeal. When Joseph Francis, munching a sandwich, made no attempt to speak, Eric came in again.

'The time of death thing is probably an ill-founded argument,' he suggested. 'In my view, and I've checked some of the authorities, it would go against the clear directions of section 7 of the Finance Act 1894.'

There was a short silence. A faint flush stained Penrose's cheek. 'You have the advantage of me, of course,' he said. 'I'm no lawyer.'

Morcomb stared coldly at Eric Ward. Joseph Francis, suddenly aware of the hostility that had crept into his client's demeanour, hurried to say, 'Well, it's a bit early to give such advice, of course. We should take counsel's opinion first on these issues, before we seriously deal with the matter of an appeal to the House of Lords. Counsel's opinion–'

'Don't forget,' Lord Morcomb remarked coldly, 'there's also the discrepancy, the marked discrepancy we would point to, between the sale price of one of the units in the Hardford Estate, achieved in 1955, and its valuation in 1971. If that individual valuation is too high, as we claim, it could affect the valuation of all the units, and that will bring down the total valuation as well. And my liability for the damned estate duty.'

There was a short silence. Joseph Francis cleared his throat. 'I don't think at this stage we need go into the details of your liability. Your accountants—'

'Damn my accountants,' Lord Morcomb snapped testily. 'This is important. My predecessor was a man of property – land and shareholdings. And he had a certain view of life. The Morcomb estates had run down to virtually nothing: the title had little to support it. My uncle was a damned good businessman and he pulled together a hell of a lot of money, a hell of a lot of land. And though it was his – not attached to the Morcomb title – he wanted it to go together. He wanted to restore the dignity of the name. Do you understand that?'

'Yes, my lord, of course, but—'

'He left it to me in his will – to me, and the heirs of my body. And I have the same ideas as he did – even though in most things, during his lifetime, we did not see eye to eye. I want the Morcomb estates, as they've been restored, to stay as much as a unit as possible, within the family. But that can't happen if half the damned money drifts away into the pockets of the Government!'

'That's an exaggeration, my lord–'

'Francis, let me put it to you clearly,' Lord Morcomb said heavily. 'I'm short of ready cash. If I'm to meet heavy death duties I have a clear choice – either I sell part of the lands now held by me, or else I start to siphon off some of the shareholdings in the portfolio that my uncle got together. I'm reluctant to do either. Share prices are depressed, and as far as the land holdings are concerned I don't want to lose them. I want them to go with my successor – my daughter, and the man she marries. But if we have to settle for the system the Commissioners suggest, damn it, it'll take a big slice from the estate.'

Paul Francis was as lost now as he had been at any time during the last two hours. He attempted to make up some ground. 'Er ... I'm not clear, my lord – the 1955 sale you referred to, a unit of the Hardford Estate?'

'The sale of Vixen Hill,' Lord Morcomb said testily, 'together with the manor house, to Colonel Denby.'

'Colonel Denby?'

Eric Ward had repeated the words before

he could control himself. The name had cropped up so unexpectedly; the Egan matter had been commanding his attention so persistently; now, hearing the name on Lord Morcomb's lips he had been unable to remain silent. He regretted his words immediately. Lord Morcomb stared at him, frowning. After a little while, he asked, 'You knew the colonel?'

Eric glanced at Joseph Francis but the senior partner was staring fixedly at his coffee cup. 'We're ... no, I didn't know Colonel Denby,' Eric said lamely. 'It's merely we're administering an estate ... a man called Egan...'

Something had happened to the atmosphere in the room. Lord Morcomb's eyes had flickered away from Ward's, so he was no longer subjected to their cold glare. But there was an almost fluorescent pallor about the old man's features suddenly, and his tight lips seemed to sag, momentarily. Ward was aware of the manner in which the veins stood out on the backs of Lord Morcomb's thin hands, and he watched as the old man carefully wiped the palms of those hands, as though they were damp. There was a short silence, then Lord Morcomb raised his head.

'Counsel's opinion, you said.' There was a

vague desperation in his husky voice, as though the contemplation of more lawyer's delays brought death that much nearer. 'All right, we'll take counsel's opinion. That will do for today, I think.'

The conference at Sedleigh Hall was over, and Lord Morcomb did not look in Ward's direction as he walked slowly from the room.

3

Joseph Francis contented himself with grunting that he'd see Ward back at the office; moments later Paul had whisked him away in his car. As Eric walked towards his own vehicle he heard steps on the gravel behind him. He looked back; it was David Penrose, taking a cigarette out of a silver case. He drew near, smiling, and offered Ward a cigarette, which he declined. 'The old man doesn't care for smoking in the house and he's got a keen nose. And after a long session like that I need a drag.' He drew on the cigarette and then cocked an eyebrow at Ward. 'You threw me a bit with that Finance Act stuff.'

Ward leaned against his car. 'I'm sorry about that. I didn't mean to blind anyone with science. I just think that if Lord Morcomb pushes that particular line he'll be ill advised.'

Penrose grinned and shrugged. 'Well, I asked for it, anyway. I was just showing off a bit, I suppose, seeking to impress my employer.' He hesitated. 'I like my job, and I'd like to keep it. Keeps me from the workhouse... So you think the time of death angle is washed out?'

'In my opinion. The authorities ... but let's get something straight,' Ward explained. 'I'm no solicitor – not yet. Still qualifying. Hack work and along for the ride, today.'

'Seems to me you knew more about issues than at least one of your companions.'

Ward made no reply. He thought it time to leave now, but Penrose seemed in no hurry to let him go. Lord Morcomb's estate manager seemed thoughtful, his eyes lidded against the cigarette smoke as he looked quizzically at Eric Ward. 'You you threw the old man a bit back there, didn't you?'

'Did I?'

'Could cut the atmosphere with a knife.' Penrose waved his cigarette negligently. 'I know Lord Morcomb; he can be hard, but he can be surprisingly vulnerable too, on occasions. And you really got to him today –

whether you meant it or not.'

'It was unintentional.'

'That's as may be ... but what's it about, anyway?'

'I wouldn't know.'

'You mentioned a name – Egan?'

'Arthur Egan. He's dead. We're administering his estate.'

'Hmmm.' Penrose considered the matter, drew again on his cigarette. 'What's the connection with Michael Denby's father, then?'

Ward stared at him. 'Michael Denby?'

'That's right. He farms from Vixen Hill now, ever since his father...' Penrose's voice died away and his glance was suddenly keen. 'His father was killed, wasn't he? I seem to remember...'

'It was Arthur Egan,' Ward said shortly. There was no reason why he should not tell Penrose; it was public knowledge anyway. 'He was convicted of the manslaughter of Colonel Denby. But I hadn't realized Denby had leased his property from Lord Morcomb.'

'That's the way of it,' Penrose replied. 'And I suppose it was a bit of a shock to Lord Morcomb, hearing the name of a man who had killed one of his tenants – even after all this time.'

It might well have been a shock, as Penrose said. But Eric Ward was left with the feeling there was more to it than that. And he suspected that David Penrose was of the same opinion. In the silence that fell, he opened the car door, and then paused. 'Exactly where is Vixen Hill?' he asked.

Penrose looked at him thoughtfully for a few moments. 'There's a track on the left, just as you reach the main road. Take it, and it'll bring you to the Sedleigh turning. Bear right there, and it's about four miles. You can't miss it – if you intend going there.'

Ward made no commitment but thanked him and got into the car. As he drove away, through the driving mirror he could see David Penrose standing there, watching him. A few moments later, as the car reached the green and the clock tower arch, the man was lost to sight.

The road was narrower than Ward had expected, even though the signpost intimated he would eventually reach the Jedburgh road. A high hedge on one side gave him no view over the fields; on the other scattered trees lurched in an overhang across the roadway, which twisted and turned every fifty yards or so.

He heard the other car long before he saw it; the driver was a careful man who sounded his horn on the bends. Ward thought it best to pull into a passing place set against the hedge rather than risk having to reverse later, and within half a minute a black Ford with a battered offside wing nosed its way around the bend ahead.

For all his caution, the other driver had miscalculated and had strayed too widely around the bend. He was forced to halt, reverse, and then swing the wheel sharply to edge towards the ditch in order to make his way past Ward. He came forward slowly; Ward waved a hand in acknowledgment, as he inched forward, but the man in the other car paid no attention. He was about forty years old, sandy-haired, his skin tanned, the hands on the wheel strong and tense. He flickered a quick glance in Ward's direction as he passed: Ward obtained a fleeting impression of eyes black as buttons, but hard and determined. Then the Ford was past him, picking up speed, and Eric was able to move forward himself.

After a mile or so the road widened, swung through a small hamlet, sturdy stone-built cottages overlooking the steep slopes of a river bank, and then ahead of him he saw another track, churned by tractor wheels but passable to a car, climbing up the slope between two fields. The sign bore the legend 'Vixen Hill' and below it, uncompromisingly, PRIVATE. Ward swung into the track and drove a little way along it, then pulled to one side, under a clump of trees. He switched off the engine, listened to the tick of cooling metal for a few minutes, deciding whether to walk over the hill and satisfy his curiosity. Then, at last, though recognizing it was merely curiosity and refusing to analyse his motivation otherwise, he got out of the car, locked it, and started to walk up the hill.

The afternoon sun was warm on his back, but the slope was gentle and he reached the brow of the hill in a matter of minutes. There the track ran over level ground for a hundred yards, then dipped sharply through some trees. Ward walked forward until he was standing on the edge of the copse.

The track ran steeply down the hillside, through birch and alder and sycamore trees, rutted, but patched here and there with stones and tarmacadam. At the bottom of the hill lay a small wooden bridge; the stream it crossed was swift-moving but shallow, the track crossing it at a ford slightly to the left of the bridge. Ward could make out a post driven into the water to record its depth; in winter, no doubt, there would be times when the bridge would be the only means of access to the other side, and when he walked down the hill he realized this would be the reason for the wooden garages standing under the trees, some fifty yards from the stream.

He walked forward and stood on the bridge. On the other side of the narrow stream the track rose to high hedges, and beyond, through the trees he could see a stone-built farmhouse – the manor house that Lord Morcomb had spoken of. It was up there that Colonel Denby had lived.

And it was on this bridge that he would have died. Ward had no idea how long he stood on the bridge, staring down into the water; his thoughts were confused and aimless. They centred on Arthur Egan, and his loneliness, but they also wandered around certain irreconcilable matters he found disturbing him. Egan had been a killer, yet the only information he had so far about the man was that there was probably only this one isolated incident of violence in his life. What had made him act in this way?

And why had Lord Morcomb reacted so oddly at the mention of his name? Surely, after twenty or more years, the name would have been forgotten.

'Can I help you?' the voice said, in a tone that suggested no desire to do any such thing.

Eric turned, startled, to see a man standing a little distance away, watching him. He had obviously come down through the trees and his boots were muddy, suggesting he had been tramping over the fields above. He was short, stocky in build, with a ruddy complexion and a fleshy mouth. He wore a battered jacket and corduroy trousers stuffed into his boots; the flat cap was set back from his wide forehead and his fair hair curled thickly at the nape of his neck.

'Er ... no, I'm sorry,' Ward said quietly. 'I ... I just came down to look at the stream, and the bridge.'

'You know this is private land?'

'I saw the sign, but ... do you live up at the manor house?'

The man came forward, thrusting his hands into the pockets of his jacket. 'That's right. I farm Vixen Hill. And I live in the manor house.'

'You must be Michael Denby.'

The stocky man came closer; his eyes were wary, and he inspected Ward's sober suit, as though suspecting he had received a visitor from the Inland Revenue. 'You're looking for me?'

'No. I said ... I just came down to look at the bridge.

But David Penrose told me a little while ago that you farmed here.'

Michael Denby's chin came up a trifle, belligerently. 'Penrose? You and he have been discussing me?'

Ward shook his head, smiling slightly. 'I'm sorry. I've not made myself very clear. I was up at Sedleigh Hall this morning, on a legal matter. Colonel – your father's name came up. Then Penrose told me you farmed here, in succession to your father. I ... I was interested in seeing ... Vixen Hill.'

Michael Denby stared at him thoughtfully for a few moments, his brow furrowed as though he was somewhat disturbed. 'A legal matter...' he murmured. 'Would that be to do with Carlton Engineering?'

Ward's lack of understanding must have shown in his face. Denby stared at him closely, then asked, 'If not that, what's your interest in Vixen Hill, then?'

Ward hesitated briefly. 'I ... I'm dealing with the administration of the estate of Arthur Egan.'

Michael Denby's expression changed subtly; his gaze became tangled, confused with conflicting reminiscences and he brushed his mouth with his hand, his breathing suddenly ragged. He stepped slowly on to the bridge, moving past Ward and he placed his stubby hands on the wooden supports. He stood quietly like that for almost a minute, staring sightlessly into the shallow stream, a man in his mid-thirties suddenly feeling much older. Then he pulled his emotions together, buried them under a faint smile as he looked at Eric Ward.

'Perhaps you'd like to come up to the house,' he said, and turned to walk across the bridge without waiting for an answer.

He was more relaxed and at ease among the Jacobean structures of his home; it was a warm house and a welcoming one, and his wife Jenny was plump, rather homely, but friendly. She bustled out to the back of the house to make a pot of tea in spite of Ward's protest that he needed none, and then Denby motioned Ward to a chair, took off his jacket and threw it on the settee, and took the chair facing Ward. He scratched his chin, slightly nervous again, and finally said, 'I asked you in because perhaps my curiosity matches – or is probably even greater – than yours.'

'How do you mean?'

'I've wondered for many years what kind of a man he was the man who killed my father.' When Ward was silent, he continued. 'Do you understand that? I never met him, never really wanted to meet him. But I wanted to know about him. And now he's dead. What kind of man was he?'

Slowly Ward said, 'I don't know that I can answer that. My essential interest is in in discovering who the beneficiaries might be to his estate. Beyond that ... I don't know, but he seems to have been a quiet, remote man, no friends, no relatives calling, cut away from his Newcastle roots and living in a semi in Westerhope and...' He hesitated, aware of the oddly hungry expression in Michael Denby's eyes. 'And maybe still brooding on the one act of gratuitous violence he seems to have committed in his life.'

A sigh escaped from Denby's lips; it could have been disappointment; it might have been frustration. 'It was an act that cost my father his life,' he said quietly.

They sat saying nothing for a moment as Jenny came in with the tea. She sensed that the conversation precluded her presence and went out, closing the door behind her. 'It's ironic, really,' Denby said, pouring the tea, 'I never knew my father's murderer, but then, I never really knew my father, either.'

He explained that he had been only twelve years old when his father had died. He had seen very little of him; a boarding school as he grew older, and before that a period spent with an aunt while his father was overseas in the Army. His mother had died when he was three. He had hero-worshipped his military father in the way a young boy would, but now, as he was older, he was trying to be more objective.

'It's why I've thought back so often to that night,' he said. 'As far as I understand things, Egan had broken into the house here – it was well known that my father had a silver collection, which has in fact now been sold – with the intention of robbing the place. My father must have heard him and came downstairs. Egan ran, taking very little of value with him. It could have ended there – Egan would presumably have been caught anyway, as he was, by selling the silver in Newcastle. But my father...' He paused ruminatively. 'Do you see how his background must have affected his decision? He took down a shotgun and went out after Egan. The questions in my mind have always been, why the hell did he chase after the man – it wasn't that important – certainly not worth throwing his

96

life away for it, at least! And Egan. Was he a violent man? Or was he just scared, panic-stricken in the darkness when my father caught up with him at the bridge, waving that shotgun in his face.'

'I gather he'd already fired one barrel,' Ward said quietly.

'And was ready to let loose with the other.' There was an edge of bitterness to his voice and Ward suspected it was directed more against his father than against the man who had killed him. But Denby's curiosity was compounded by not really knowing either man, yet seeing the incident in his mind's eye, over and over again. 'After my father died, my aunt and uncle came to run the farm for a few years, and I came home from school. Eventually, I took over the lease. But almost every time I walk across that bridge...' He glanced at Ward shamefacedly. 'You'd think that kind of thing would have faded over the years, but it hasn't. The stupidity of it all. Egan, scrabbling away with a few trivial pieces of silver; my father, chasing him with a shotgun, and prepared to use it, for God's sake! You know, I think I would have acted the way Egan did. One of the stanchions of the bridge was broken. He grabbed it up and hit out at my father. But then, when my father was down, why did he hit him again? The trial ... the newspapers said he'd hit him three times.'

It would have been touch and go with a self-defence plea, Ward thought as Denby sat brooding. One blow, sending Colonel Denby to his knees ... Egan should have run, then. Instead, he had struck at the prostrate man, twice more. Maybe Francis, Shaw and Elder had done a better job with the defence than Joe Francis suggested.

'You didn't really explain why you came to Vixen Hill,' Denby said after a little while. 'Was it just curiosity?'

'I suppose so,' Ward replied. 'I know very little about Arthur Egan – he kept very much to himself. I don't even know yet where he was working in this district. It was some-where around here, wasn't it?'

'Oh yes,' Michael Denby nodded. 'He worked at Seddon Burn, about eight miles from here. There was a hall there – it burned down about ten or fifteen years ago now, and the chap who leased it from Lord Morcomb emigrated, I believe. But it was he who em-ployed Arthur Egan. He ran the stables – there was quite a fine stable there, I seem to remember. Mainly hunting, of course, but I seem to recall he also had some racing bloodstock. That's where Egan was, anyway.'

Ward was puzzled. 'Odd thing to do, some-how, wasn't it?'

Michael Denby watched him for a little while. He knew what he meant. He scratched his cheek thoughtfully. 'Like I said, I know nothing about Egan, but I was always a bit puzzled. There was never any talk about why he broke into the house that night. Bits of silver, yes ... but he had a good job, so why commit a burglary? And it seems it was the only such act he ever committed.'

'The only act of burglary, the only act of violence.' Ward nodded. 'A man working in the country, having escaped the terraces of Byker and Scotswood. And more-over, he commits the robbery so close to home.'

There was something wrong about it. He felt it in his bones. Policemen often worked on instinct, and were suitably criticized for it when they failed to produce evidence to confirm their suspicions, but Eric Ward had never discounted instinct. He was no longer a policeman, but his instincts had not changed, and there was something wrong about the events of that night. But it was a long time ago, and most of the people con-cerned were dead.

'There is one thing,' he said after finishing

his cup of tea. 'You say Egan worked at Seddon Burn. Is there a village there?'

'Of sorts.'

'Did you ever hear any rumours about Egan fathering a child on one of the local girls? You see, the problem is, in his instructions to us he wrote of a child or grand-children. He was a lonely, remote man, and at the end racked with cancer, and he might have been fantasizing – maybe he never had a child. We're advertising, with no response so far. But I just wondered...'

Michael Denby was shaking his head. 'I've heard no rumour ... but then, it's not likely I would. But if you like, I'll ask around, because I go to one of the locals occasionally, and there's a group of old men there who seem to know about almost everything that's happened in these hills for the last fifty years.'

'I'm grateful.' Ward rose, walked through to the kitchen to thank Jenny Denby, and then Michael Denby walked down the track to the bridge with him. They shook hands there, and Ward turned to go when Denby sud-denly raised his hand to his eyes, shading them as he stared past Ward to the trees on the hillside. Eric Ward looked back, and saw the horse and rider picking their way through the trees and down the track towards them.

The horse was a magnificent animal, sheer black, with muscles that rippled under its glossy coat. It held its head high, spiritedly, and there was a nervous energy in its pacing that suggested tremendous power and urgency. The rider was a young woman, in her early twenties, dressed in riding habit. She rode with an elegant, practised ease and she raised one hand to wave to Michael Denby. As she drew nearer Denby led Ward across the bridge. He smiled; the girl drew near and dismounted, caressing the black's nose, and then she grinned up at Michael Denby. 'Thought I'd call in as I was going past. See you and Jenny – haven't been around for a while. David prefers the ride over Stagshaw Fell, but he had to cry off today so I took my favourite old ride.'

'I'm pleased you did so,' Denby replied. 'And Jenny'll be delighted to see you. Er ... you won't have met Eric Ward.'

'No.' She turned to look up at him and he realized she was quite small. She held out her hand; it was light-boned, but strong, and the grip was firm and friendly. Her face was regular in features, her mouth smiling, her eyes wide-spaced. She was not beautiful in a formal way, but there was a liveliness in her manner that appealed to him. 'I'm Anne

Morcomb,' she announced.

The surprise must have shown in his eyes, for her smile widened. 'What's the matter?' she asked. 'We haven't met before, have we?'

'No, it's not that. It's just that I have just come from Lord Morcomb's home–'

'Ahh.' She flicked an interested glance over him. 'You'll be one of the people Daddy was seeing this morning about the estate. A solicitor?'

'Almost.'

'How do you be an almost solicitor?'

Eric Ward explained about articled clerks, but very much aware she was looking at him and noting his age, in an uncritical way, however. 'So don't tell me you came down to Michael's to investigate his title, or something.'

Denby grinned. 'I thought he'd come down about Carlton Engineering.'

She shook her head emphatically. 'I'll never let Daddy open up Vixen Hill for that company.' She caught the puzzlement in Ward's eyes, and went on. 'Carlton Engineering are a company in some kind of consortium which wants to develop open-cast mining in the area. I'm completely against it – and so is Michael. It would simply ruin the area, which is mainly agricultural, and the scheme would

make it necessary to construct several road-
ways which would change the whole character of the estates. One of the roads would
have to cut behind Vixen Hill, you see, effectively splitting Michael's farm in two. They've
made several offers to Daddy, and officers
from the Department of the Environment
keep ringing him up. It's all very unpleasant.
There's a much simpler answer, and that is to
release no land if Daddy has to pay this estate
duty thing, but raise the money by selling
shares instead. Still, all this is beside the
point. If it's not Michael's title, and not
Carlton Engineering, what legal matter does
bring you down here? I'm the original
curious cat, you know,' she added, smiling.

Eric Ward told her, briefly. Her glance
slipped to Michael, still not understanding.

'Arthur Egan was the man who killed my
father,' he explained.

She said nothing for a moment, but just
looked at him sympathetically, and Ward
realized that she was aware of the conflicts
that had lain inside Michael Denby over the
years. She turned back to Ward. 'But what
did you expect to find on Vixen Hill, as far
as this man Egan's estate is concerned?'

'Nothing really. It was ... curiosity that drew
me here. And, well, as it, happens I've also

103

now found out where Egan worked. It was at Seddon Burn–'

'I know it. It's my old ride – it takes me past it. I came that way this afternoon. Creepy place now, really. Burned out shell.' She paused thoughtfully. 'It's spoiled the ride in one sense; in another, I suppose it hasn't. From the hill it looks kind of romantic. But I'd rather have had the ride the way it was when Mother used to take it. However...'

'Mr Ward essentially wants to know whether Egan had an affair with one of the local girls,' Denby interrupted. 'He's having some trouble tracing Egan's relatives.'

'Well, I'm sure I wouldn't know about that,' Anne Morcomb said, laughing. 'Anyway, I'll go in to see Jenny. Nice to meet you, Mr Ward. Perhaps we'll see each other again, sometime.'

'I hope so,' he said, meaning it, and was then slightly disturbed to realize she had caught the nuance. Her eyes held his for a moment and she smiled faintly, then turned away, leading the black through the ford. They watched her as she went; as she reached the far bank she looked back, raised her hand. 'Just occurred to me,' she called. 'The local girls thing. If anyone knows about it, it'll be old Sarah Boden. Remember her,

Michael? She worked for Daddy for a while, I believe, but her last years of service were as housekeeper at Seddon Burn. A local woman, with a fund of local knowledge. I should try her, Mr Ward. I believe she lives up at Warkworth, now. Anyway, good luck in your search.'

Michael Denby watched her affectionately as she led her horse up the track towards the farmhouse. When she was out of sight, Ward asked, 'Have you known her long?'

'Forever, seems to me,' Denby said, smiling again. 'She was a frequent visitor when she was a child. You see, her mother – she was Lord Morcomb's second wife – died when Anne was about five or six, and somehow or other my aunt used to contrive to bring her over from the big house to spend time here. I don't think I enjoyed her company too much then – I was at an age when girls were not my scene at all! – but she still comes over to visit from time to time; I'm very fond of her. I'm glad she...' He hesitated, glanced at Ward, then shrugged. 'Her mother, Elizabeth Morcomb, died of a thrombosis. Very sudden. She gave her looks to Anne but not, thank the Lord, her general manner.'

'How do you mean?'

'Difficult to explain, really. She never

seemed happy. You had the feeling there was a sort of intensity with her, a pent-up frustration of some kind. And she seemed perennially unhappy ... sort of moody. I didn't see much of her, of course, and when she was with Anne she was lively and happy enough. But there was something, something odd about her. I sensed it. Still...'He frowned. 'What was the name of the woman Anne mentioned, again?'

'Sarah Boden.'

'Mmmm. And you'll try to see her?'

'I'll try. But it won't be for a few days, I'm afraid. The firm can't revolve around the affairs of Arthur Egan!'

'I don't suppose it can,' Denby said softly and made a gesture of goodbye as Eric Ward turned and began the climb back to the top of the hill and the car awaiting him beside the hedge above.

Chapter Three

1

During the next few days Eric Ward found his thoughts constantly returning to the girl he had met at Vixen Hill. At first he made no attempt to analyse the impression she had made upon him; later, as he found her image presenting itself again and again to his mind he tried to consider what it was that he found attractive about her. It still gave no explanation why he should be thinking of her so often.

And he was almost twice her age.

He saw nothing of Joseph Francis during this time, and in the two occasions Paul met him on the stairs he was brusque and surly. Ward guessed that Joseph had given his son a lecture concerning his performance at Sedleigh Hall. Paul made no attempt, nevertheless, to recover the Morcomb file, which still lay on Eric's desk, and after he had dealt with the work outstanding on his desk Eric opened the file and extracted a map of the estates owned by Lord Morcomb, and provided for the devious purposes of the Inland Revenue Commissioners.

As he inspected the map he wondered precisely where Carlton Engineering wanted to establish their open-cast mining operations: by following the contours delineated on the map, he could make an educated guess about the roadway which Anne Morcomb had mentioned at Vixen Hill, and it would certainly carve away a huge slice of the farmland presently leased by Michael Denby. He returned to the file and began to read sections of the evidence presented to the Inland Revenue Commissioners, recalling something Anne Morcomb had said. He soon discovered the necessary schedules: it seemed that when the previous Lord Morcomb had died, the trust he had established by his will in favour of his successor and his heirs had included not only the land comprising the Morcomb estates, but also a considerable shareholding. Surprisingly, the portfolio did not include many different shares – there were only half-a-dozen separate companies nominated. The holdings, nevertheless, were large.

His thoughts drifted back to Carlton Engineering. He presumed it was a limited company, but he wondered at its name – he would have expected a company interested in open-cast mining to have a name more closely connected with the mining industry. A half hour's diligent searching gave him the answer. Carlton Engineering Ltd was a subsidiary, specializing in earth-moving equipment, of another company called Western Consolidated Mining Ltd, who were in turn merely a member company of a holding operation called Western Enterprises Ltd. Eric Ward guessed that the Carlton Engineering offers to Lord Morcomb would therefore be in the nature of a wide-ranging deal at the end of the day between the subsidiary companies, each of whom might have a stake in the final mining and reconstruction undertakings.

And they could very well get what they wanted, he considered, as he looked back again at the details specified in Lord Morcomb's struggle with the Inland Revenue. Either way, his lordship would be forced to pay heavy death duties; when he was called upon to do so, that extra half million or so he was disputing with the Commissioners could force him to raise ready cash – by the sale of land or shares.

He had some sympathy with Anne Morcomb's views – he hoped that his lordship would dispense with his shares rather than his land.

As he was closing the file the telephone rang.

'A gentleman called Mr Parton to speak to you,' the switchboard girl told him.

'Put him on, please.'

A buzz and then he heard Jackie Parton's voice. 'Eric? You going to be busy this evening?'

'Not particularly. Why?'

'Got someone you ought to have a chat with.'

'Have you picked up some information on the Egan administration?'

'Tell you this evening. Six-thirty, at the Hydraulic Engine, down on Scotswood. Okay? See you then.'

Mud flats lay exposed at the bend of the river, which glinted greyly under a dark evening sky. The boats that lay stranded on the mud had a depressing, bedraggled look, as though, beached by the tide, they despaired of ever seeing the sea again. A scrap-iron yard abutting on the shore gave exit to a late, snarling lorry as Eric Ward pulled in to one side and parked his car. Across the roadway, almost opposite the yard and the mud flats of the Tyne, was the Hydraulic Engine.

It was a large, square, cream-painted building with red-bricked windows and a green slate roof. On one side of the public house was a decaying sailor's mission; on the other, the Tyneside Irish Club, with a faded shamrock painted on its door. It meant, Ward knew, that the Hydraulic Engine did a roaring trade of a certain kind – particularly on a Saturday night.

He had visited the pub several times as a policeman, but never since he left the Force. He found now a certain pleasure in avoiding the thinly veiled hostility that had previously greeted his entrance: even out of uniform, he had still been recognized as a jack. Now, not a head turned as he entered.

Jackie Parton was sitting with two or three tables to his left, at which a group of men, with pints in front of them, carried on a jocular conversation with him. As Ward came forward Parton rose and walked towards him, drew him to one side behind a glass partition screen beside the bar. He ordered Ward a half pint of lager, obtained another beer for himself, then sat down.

'Thought it was better meeting here than elsewhere. Some hot-house orchids don't flourish away from their reg' lar environment.'

'What's that supposed to mean?'

Jackie Parton exposed his teeth in a grimace that masqueraded as a smile. 'Got someone you should meet, and talk to. Suspect he wouldn't say much elsewhere – if he'd even turn up. You might say he's a very suspicious individual. He'll be along shortly.'

'And till then?'

'We'll have a little drink, and I'll make my report to you – along with a claim for some expenses.'

Ward sipped his lager. He'd thought, when warned off by George Knox, the police surgeon, that he would really miss drink of an alcoholic nature. He hadn't. No smoking; no drinking; no tension. But life wasn't bad – except for the pain. He looked around the bar at the ill-clad, loud-mouthed inhabitants of the Hydraulic Engine and knew things could be worse. 'All right, Jackie, what have you got?'

The little man screwed up his eyes and took another drink. 'Well, I'll tell you, not a lot. This chap Arthur Egan, he's not an easy feller to get information on. I've talked to a lot of people around Scotswood and Byker way now, and the ones who knew him, or of him, they're not so numerous. His going off to Northumberland–'

'Seddon Burn.'

'Oh yeah? You been working yourself, then? Anyway, him going off there, then prison, then this quiet life in Westerhope, it's left him a pretty colourless character, with not many leads. He's still remembered by a few, and they all say the same two things about him: he was a handsome lad, and he was a quiet feller. Not one I've spoken to says he had a wild temper.'

'And?'

'And not one of them says he had a thing for the women.'

'So he wasn't a high liver. That still doesn't mean he didn't have anyone,' Ward said, slightly exasperated.

'But that's the talk.' Jackie Parton insisted. 'He didn't have anyone. He was a loner. In Scotswood; in Byker; in Westerhope; it's always the same tale. He just didn't seem interested in women. Polite; courteous; but not interested.'

Ward sighed. 'So what do you conclude from that?' Jackie Patton put one foot on the stool in front of him and lit himself a cigarette. 'My conclusions are pretty simple. It's all a fantasy. There isn't any kid. There aren't any grandkids. There may be relatives – but only may be. But you're asking me to find a child is moonshine, a waste of money. I think Egan was drifting, pain – drugged, lonely: I think he manufactured a family out of his head.'

Eric Ward had already suspected as much. Everything was pointing to it; the man's life style underpinned it. 'You said there may be other relatives.'

Parton drew on his cigarette. 'Could be. This brother of his ... well, half-brother really. Andrews, Tommy Andrews. Now he was a bit younger than Egan and though he went to sea just about when Egan was working at those stables, and though nothing's seemed to have been heard of him since, there's a chance he's still alive. If not him, maybe his kids. I presume if he had kids, they could come into Egan's money?'

'If there were no closer relatives.'

'Well, I'm still asking around, then. But it's not going to be easy. These two lads ... they were chalk and cheese, you know.'

'How do you mean?' Ward asked.

Parton waved his cigarette in a vague gesture, encompassing most of the men in the bar. 'Takes all sorts, don't it? And in one

114

family alone you can get very different brothers. These two were only half-brothers, of course, but they had little in common, so I'm told. That doesn't mean they weren't close, you understand – but Tommy was a spoiled kid, it seems. He got into a lot of scrapes as a youngster, and it was usually left to Egan to drag him out of them. And he certainly squired it around a bit when he was older – if Arthur Egan didn't go much on the birds, young Tommy certainly did. So, chances are he'll have left some part of himself lying around in Newcastle, even if Arthur didn't. For that matter, maybe it was one of Tommy's kids Egan had in mind.'

'You'll keep asking around?'

'I've a few more contacts... This Andrews character, though, I wonder about him. He was quite a tearaway, I think – they don't talk that way among the terraces about someone unless he really was wild. And I've got a kind of feeling about him, you know, Eric? I feel he's going to turn up, one of these days.' He grinned suddenly. 'And maybe I won't like it when he does. Some people don't like having questions asked about them!'

Ward grunted, knowing what he meant. He glanced at his watch. 'When's this man you want me to meet turning up?'

'He already did, about five minutes ago. He's over there, at the corner of the bar.'

The man was of medium height, square-set, but stooping arthritically. He wore a large Army greatcoat, several sizes too big for him and at the throat a thick pullover, greasy and stained, with a ragged neck, was gaping. His hair was long, his beard spiky and it was several moments before Eric Ward remembered where he had seen him before. It was all of ten years or more, in a small pawnshop near the quayside. A dark room, a querulous but frightened man, stolen goods and an eagerness to cooperate when pressure was applied. 'Tiggy Williams,' Eric Ward said quietly.

'The very same,' Parton agreed, and one corner of his scarred mouth lifted. 'I think you ought to buy him a drink.'

Tiggy Williams was in no hurry to join them; indeed, it required some persuasion from Jackie Parton, and it was only the promise of several drinks, Ward suspected, that brought the man across to their table. Parton pushed him down into a chair, and said, 'You remember Mr Ward, don't you Tiggy?'

Suspicious eyes flickered a nervous glance in Ward's direction; they could not hold Ward's glance and flickered away again.

'Don't like drinkin' with coppers,' he said.
'I'm not a copper,' Ward said quietly.

'You was a copper when–'

'I've left the Force now. I'm working with a solicitor.' Tiggy Williams looked relieved, but only slightly so: solicitors were obviously not to be trusted either. He brightened visibly, however, when Parton put a pint of Scotch Ale in front of him. He drank deeply from it, and froth stained his spiky beard. Ward suddenly remembered the library at Sedleigh Hall and looked around him at the grimy interior of the Hydraulic Engine. They were worlds apart, and suddenly impatient, he glared at Jackie Parton.

'Well?'

The ex-jockey raised an eyebrow at Ward's impatience, then shrugged. 'As you know, I've been asking around. The other day I called in on old Tiggy, here. We got chatting, and at the end he had an interesting story to tell.'

'No stories,' Tiggy Williams muttered.

Jackie Parton smiled engagingly. 'Oh, come on, Tiggy, all friends here. And no comeback.'

'I don't know,' Williams muttered, and finished his Scotch. Parton rose and bought him another; the old man did not look up to meet Ward's eyes. When Parton returned he put the fresh pint down and said, 'Thing was, Eric, as you ask around one thing leads to another. I thought I'd try to find out if this woman called Meg Salter could help us in our enquiries. She gave evidence at Arthur Egan's trial. She was the one – a dairymaid – who saw Egan burning bloodstained clothing after Colonel Denby died. Didn't get to see her; died a few years back, but had a long chat with her son. He told me Meg Salter always had a conscience about giving that evidence: apparently she liked Arthur Egan a lot. Bit sweet on him, it seems – she was a widow at the time – but he always kept pretty much to himself. But she saw him burn that clothing all right, and when the police came to her she told them. But she always felt sorry she'd done it; sorry for Egan. But Tiggy here, he wasn't sorry, were you, hey?'

'Doing my duty,' Tiggy Williams muttered.

'Duty my backside,' Parton said affably. 'Your motives were quite different, from what you told me the other night.'

Tiggy Williams was nervous. He looked uneasily at Jackie Parton, then at Ward, and then back to Parton again. 'You said there was no need–'

'No need for it to go any further, no

further than my friend here, is what I said,'
Parton soothed him. 'But what you worried
about? Egan's dead. I told you so. There's
no hassle; no problem. So you can tell us,
can't you? You already told me, anyway – so
just tell Mr Ward here, now.'

'I was caught clear, you see, that was the
problem,' Tiggy Williams said, in a self-
justifying whine.

'I don't understand,' Ward said, leaning
forward.

'It was a bloke off one of the ships at the
Quayside. We got talking in the boozer, and
he said he knew where he could get his
hands on some of the stuff. Snow.'

'Cocaine?' Ward said unbelievingly.

'That's right. Oh, I know, it wasn't my
thing. I mean, drugs is something I never...
But this seemed to be too good to miss. It
was two hundred quid, just to pass it on to
some lads at the coast. I'd just be the go-
between. And I swear I never even got my
hands on the stuff. Next thing I know was
that this bloke didn't turn up. He'd been
hauled in, as he left the ship. They canned
him, then two days later I got hauled in as
well. And they really put the screws on me.'

'What kind of screws?'

The beady eyes took on a cunning glint.

'Come on Mr. Ward, you know all about that. They had a list of things – stuff that got pulled from various jobs. They was going to say it all came through me. All right, I was a fence, I'm admittin' that – don't do no more now, mind you – but I had a record and I took stuff. But this list, I mean it was just rubbish, wasn't it! And then I was pulled in for a private talk with the Super. And he laid it on the line. They was going to fix me with the snow job as well. I'd have been put away a long time on that, I tell you–'

'But you said you didn't receive the cocaine – the seaman didn't turn up.'

'That's the truth!' Cunning was replaced by earnestness. 'Never saw him; never touched the stuff. But they'd pulled him in, and the Super said I'd get booked as well. It'd take just a grain, he said.'

Ward hesitated. 'You mean they were going to plant a grain of cocaine on you and book you as being tied in with the smuggler?'

'That was it.'

Ward watched the old man for a moment. A faint odour of decay seemed to emanate from him and he wrinkled his nose in disgust. 'But you didn't get booked, Tiggy, is that it?'

'I didn't get booked. I got offered a deal,

instead.' Ward could see it coming. 'Tell me about it.'

'The Super took me in this room and he closed the door and he said we got this bastard and we got him cold but juries can be awkward buggers and we need just a bit of evidence to make the whole thing water-tight and all I had to do was say this bloke had come into my pawnshop and tried to pawn a ring and some silver and I handed it over to the coppers and then they'd be asking me to take an identification parade. You got to understand, Mr Ward, I was scared: they had a whole book to throw at me, and this snow thing–'

'How did they fix the parade?' Ward asked, feeling slightly sick.

'There was no real problem. They had them in this room and I got this feller pointed out to me. Then they went out in the yard and lined 'em up and I went out and put the finger on him. And that was that. I got spruced up when I went to court later, but that was that – I gave the story and it went along quiet enough.'

'The man was Arthur Egan?'

'That's right.'

'Had he ever come into your pawnshop?'

'Hell, no, never seen him before that

parade.' Tiggy finished his Scotch Ale and looked hopefully at the two men sitting with him. Neither moved.

'Why now, Tiggy? Why not years ago?' Ward asked in disgust.

'What for? Hell, if I'd spoken up at the time I'd have got throwed inside myself! And later ... Egan might've come for me. I was scared a while after he came out, but he never came looking for me. And now ... well, I heard Jackie was askin' around, and there's no edge, is there? The old bugger's dead now, and they're gone, nearly all of them, so no hassle.'

Eric Ward's lips were dry. He was remembering a previous conversation, in another pub. 'Tell me, Tiggy, who was the Super who took you into the room and persuaded you?'

Tiggy Williams managed a malicious grin. 'Him? Oh, he was a hard bastard, that one. Knew how to put the screws on all right. But you know something else? I reckon he was being screwed too. I tell you, he wanted me to finger Egan bad. He was sweating, and usually it's the poor little sod like me who does the sweating.'

'Who was it, Tiggy?'

'Starling. You know, him that became Chief Constable, later.'

2

The question was, did it really matter?

Jackie Patton was noncommittal about it all. His attitude was that he was being paid to dig out information – and if what he discovered was not exactly the information required by Eric Ward, that wasn't his fault. He'd managed to discover very little that might lead Ward to the beneficiaries of the estate, but he had certainly raised other problems.

Ward sat in his office the following morning with the Egan file open in front of him. An immense depression gripped him; he felt he was in danger of moving into matters that were irrelevant and damaging. It was no business of his to learn whether or not the retired Chief Constable had been guilty of forging evidence and worse, over twenty years ago. It was not his affair to discover why it had been felt necessary to push Egan to trial on evidence that, according to ex-Detective Inspector Kenton, could well have been planted. It was possible the police had then worked on the same instincts that had often motivated Eric Ward: they had known

Egan had killed Denby, but the evidence was thin, so they had 'arranged' matters.

But did it now really matter? Egan was dead; the events twenty years old and more; the Chief Constable a farmer near Jedburgh and among the hunting set he had yearned to join for years; what was to be gained by raking over these old, dying coals?

There had been no replies to the advertisement, apart from some obvious fortune-hunting ones which could be easily disposed of, and he was no nearer to finding the beneficiaries of the Egan estate than he had been at the beginning. What was worse, he was beginning to become obsessed with matters of no relevance to his basic enquiries, and that was bad.

Vaguely dissatisfied, Ward opened the envelope again and looked at the lock of blond hair. He wondered how long Arthur Egan had kept it. Then the photographs:

Egan with Tommy Andrews. The baby ... was it Egan's child, or, as was more likely, was it a photograph of Tommy as a baby?

And then the grave, and the churchyard. Perhaps the answer lay there.

The phone rang. The switchboard girl explained it was a Mr Michael Denby. He said he'd made some enquiries, and come across a man who had befriended Arthur Egan after he had come out of prison. It might be useful to interview him. He lived in a cottage on the Hardford Estate.

His name was Bridges. Fred Bridges.

After Denby had rung off Ward took the letter out of the file again, and read the last few lines.

'So, watch how you go, lad, and good luck. And no more nonsense, hey? Yours sincerely Fred.'

There were various matters to be dealt with in the office before Ward could get away; Paul Francis had pushed some more files in his direction and he needed to ensure that they contained matters he could deal with at home later. By lunchtime, however, he was clear enough to leave the office and drive north again. It was a sunny afternoon, and the roads were fairly quiet, so he made good time. He decided he'd call in to see Michael Denby first, before driving on to the Hardford Estate to see Bridges.

On this occasion Ward ran the car down the track and parked near the garages, before crossing the stream and walking up to the house. He found Denby out at the back, in the small orchard, sawing wood. He was stripped to the waist in the warm afternoon, and his heavily muscled body glistened with sweat, while his ruddy complexion was now glowing as the result of his exertions.

'I really came to thank you for your help, and to ask just who this man Bridges is, before I go to see him.'

Denby ran a massive forearm across his forehead. 'I came across his name up at the local pub the other evening, and was introduced to him afterwards. He wasn't all that keen to talk, but in the end he did admit he knew Egan after he came out of jug. He's retired now, but he was a gamekeeper for Lord Morcomb for years, apparently. That's how he came to meet Egan. Arrested him, it seems.'

'*Arrested* him?'

'Poaching, of all things,' Denby said, shaking his head slowly. 'It all seems a bit odd, but Bridges got to like Egan and somehow or other the charges were dropped and Bridges apparently helped Egan get a decent job. But no doubt he'll tell you himself. Drink before you go?'

Ward refused, explaining he had better get on because he had it in mind to call in at Warkworth on the way back, to try to see the

woman Anne Morcomb had mentioned –
Sarah Boden. 'And after that, well, I think
we're just going to have to wind up the estate
quickly. I don't see much hope of tracing
Egan's relatives. It's not been long, but there
are too many dead ends.'

'Well, anything I can do to help.'

He took some further directions from
Denby and then went back to his car. A
twenty-minute drive through winding back
lanes brought him to the tiny hamlet where
Fred Bridges had his cottage. It was neat,
sprucely-kept, with a white-painted wicker
gate and trailing ivy all along its front.
Rather twee for Ward's taste, he could yet
understand a man wishing to spend his
declining years in such a quiet spot.

Not that Fred Bridges was ready to decline
yet. When he stood in the open doorway he
filled it. He was perhaps sixty-six years of age,
over six feet tall, with a shock of grey hair, a
deep, massive chest, and long, powerfully
muscled arms. His face was the colour and
texture of leather, his mouth grim, his attitude a no-nonsense one. Ward could understand how he might have ruled the Morcomb
estates and their shooting rights with a rod of
iron: he looked the kind of man who would
have beaten the hell out of a poacher rather

than taken him to the magistrates.

'You'll be the gentleman Mr Denby spoke of; the one making enquiries about Arthur Egan.'

He spoke with the curling Northumberland 'rr' in his throat, and his directness suggested their interview would be short – particularly since, rather than invite Ward into the cottage, the man stepped outside and sat down on the low stone wall in the sunshine, waiting for Ward to put his questions.

Having briefly explained the purpose of his enquiries, Eric Ward said, 'I gather you became friendly with Egan some time after he came out of prison.'

'Matter of months after he was released, I recall,' Bridges said laconically.

'And I gather you met him in a ... er ... professional capacity?'

'You mean I catched him poaching, don't you. Yes, something like that.'

'He wasn't prosecuted,' Ward remarked.

Fred Bridges stared at him without expression for almost a minute. He seemed to be calculating, weighing his words, preparing, discarding, sorting out phrases he might use. In the silence Ward heard from across the valley a car starting up, distant, out of place in the warm hamlet where Bridges lived.

'I'll tell you how it was,' Bridges said abruptly. 'In my job with Lord Morcomb I was responsible for trampin' most of the Hardford Estate. But poachers, they don't keep to boundaries. And there's some roads they take where they can be catched easy as a wink, if you knows where. But it meant me and my squad, we worked better movin' off Hardford. So his lordship had this agreement with those leasin' properties on the Hardford boundaries that I could move on them and take poachers if I caught them. They'd go along with the prosecutions after.' He snapped off a budding rose from the bush beside him and inspected it critically for greenfly. Fancifully, Ward thought he detected the same game-keeping glint in the man's eye as would have been present all the many nights in the woods. 'Anyway,' Bridges continued, 'I knew at this time that someone new and clumsy was abroad. Couple of times I heard him; saw him once. Couldn't be sure he was taking anything, particularly since his timing was odd. Dusk, like, not late on in the dark. So I went up one afternoon and watched and waited, and I saw him in the lane and I followed him, other side of the hedge. In the dusk he slipped into the woods. So I went in and got him. Told him I knew he was a poacher, and said I'd beat hell out of him if I ever caught him with a bird.'

'What did he say in answer?'

'Nothing. Just stood there. Mind, if he'd have turned nasty, I'd have beaten the hell out of him.'

'So what happened then?' Ward asked.

'Few days later, caught him again. But different this time. I found a brace of pheasant with their necks snapped, and I confronted him with them, told him I had him by the short and curlies this time.'

'And–?'

'Took him back to my place.' Fred Bridges looked away from Ward suddenly as though he didn't want Ward to see his face. His hands were still, as though a certain tension had crept into his veins. 'We had a talk,' he said abruptly. 'And I decided I wouldn't hand him over to the magistrates. You see, them pheasants, I couldn't prove he'd took them. Some other night lad might've done it and been scared off by Egan's blundering. And Egan said he didn't know nothing about the birds. So I didn't know what to believe. Anyway, I asked him about himself and he said he was just out of prison and had no job and I took a shine to him, took pity on him if you like. We had a few drinks together, and he seemed a good enough bloke, so I got his address from him and then a few days later I got in touch with a friend of mine and fixed Egan up with a job. Market gardener. He stayed there, I'm told, rest of his working life.'

'Did you keep in touch with him?'

'No.'

'Did you write this letter to him?' Ward extracted the letter from the file and held it out to Bridges. The man stiffened, turned slowly. He seemed very reluctant to look at the letter; he handled it gingerly, with an inexplicable tension. Then, after a moment he seemed to relax. He handed it back. 'No date on it. But I wrote it. Must've been when I fixed him up in Stanley. Yeh, that's my letter.'

Ward stared at Bridges with a feeling of disappointment. Somehow, he had expected more than this. He put the letter back in the file. 'I thought ... I'd hoped you might have had a longer, more friendly relationship with Egan.'

'No. That was all there was to it.'

Ward hesitated. There was something odd about Bridges's tale, something that seemed to leave questions unanswered. 'You took a bit of a chance, didn't you?' he asked after a short silence.

'About what?'

'Writing to an acquaintance about a job for someone you'd only known a short time.'

'I liked him,' Bridges replied shortly.

'But you'd met him under pretty strange circumstances – walking the woods, maybe poaching. And then he told you he'd just come out of prison. I mean, they're hardly recommendations, are they? What made you–'

'I was sorry for him.' Fred Bridges rose to his feet and half turned his back on Eric Ward. He surveyed the quiet street of the hamlet as though Ward were no longer with him. A hard man, a strong, self-sufficient man, not the kind of individual who would be given to philanthropic gestures of any kind to a stranger he found prowling his estates.

'I find your conduct difficult to understand, Mr Bridges,' Ward said quietly.

The ex-gamekeeper made no reply for a moment. Then he turned, slowly, and glared at Ward. They were much of a height and Bridges had allowed resentment to seep into his eyes. 'I don't really give a damn what you think, friend. But that's the way it was.'

Ward was puzzled. The man was uneasy, and angry – yet he stayed, even now. He did not want to answer Ward's questions, yet he

132

stayed. 'And you never saw Egan again, or talked to him?'

'No.'

'So you knew very little about him, then? You wouldn't know, for instance, whether he ever had any sort of liaison with one of the girls around here?'

'Our acquaintance was short. We talked; but we didn't talk about women.'

He stood there, heavy, waiting, impatient. Ward felt the man was holding something back, or else was tensed for another question he did not want to answer. The silence between them grew, deepened, increased in tension. At last, with an unpleasant snorting noise, Bridges hawked and spat, and then turned and walked towards the door of the cottage. In his view, the interview was over.

'Mr Bridges, tell me,' Ward suddenly asked of the broad, retreating back, 'You said you caught Egan in the woods, but you implied it wasn't in woods on the Hardford Estate. Just where did you find him?'

Bridges hesitated in his stride; he didn't want to turn, but he did. A muscle jerked in his jaw. 'Over there.' He gestured vaguely.

'Where?' Ward pressed him. Bridges made no reply. Afterwards, Eric Ward could only think it was pure instinct that made him ask

133

the question, for there was no essential reason that he should have thought of the location. But ask it he did.

'The woods you caught Egan in,' he said. 'Were they the woods above Colonel Denby's farm?' When Bridges made no reply, Ward insisted, 'It was Vixen Hill, wasn't it? That's where you caught him.'

There was still no reply but Ward knew from the expression on Fred Bridges's face that his surmise had been correct.

3

The discussion with Bridges had been briefer and less productive than Ward had hoped for. Equally, it had compounded some of the problems that had been bothering him. It was as though Egan was taking over his thoughts and his actions, driving him along an old, dusty track from which the footprints of earlier walkers had long been erased by time.

And central to it was Vixen Hill.

It was there that Arthur Egan had tried to rob Colonel Denby; there the colonel had lost his life. But what possible magnetic attraction had the farm held for Arthur Egan

134

– to be drawn to it to kill, and as a result serve a prison sentence, and then to be drawn back to it, not once, according to Fred Bridges, but several times?

And then, apparently, after the job offer in Stanley, nothing. Instead, a quiet, uneventful life in Westerhope, lonely, reclusive, until cancer gripped him and maybe sent fanciful images into his brain about a family that had never existed.

Yet Ward knew something was missing. A piece of the puzzle remained to be fitted, and the answer lay at Vixen Hill.

As he drove, he was preoccupied, and it was perhaps two miles from Vixen Hill before he realized he had taken a wrong turning. The lane was narrow and it was necessary to continue before he could find a turning place. In the event he was forced to drive for almost a mile further before he saw a side road. He pulled in, intending to reverse and go back the way he had come; instead, as he saw the sign itself, he changed his mind. It proclaimed SEDDON BURN.

The narrow road looped over the hill, dipping into folds in the ground and zigzagging past open fields, following the track of a stream that wound its unhurried way through small farms and meadows. Some two miles ahead of him a tree-lined hill rose and he suspected that the village would lie at its foot; in fact, he discovered that the village lay beyond the crest, a scattering of houses, a Norman church and one village store. He drove on, descending, and then as he swung left he saw beyond the moss-grown stone wall the burned-out remains of Seddon Burn Hall.

The house had stood under the shelter of the hill, but commanding a southerly aspect across the village and towards the rolling hills of Northumberland. It was approached by a long, curving drive flanked by elms and rhododendron; now, in the years since the hall had been destroyed the elm trees had died too, stricken by disease, while the rhododendron had flourished, spilling across the driveway in a tangle of green from which the stark trunks of the elms stood accusingly. To drive up there would be impossible; Ward parked the car, and thrust his way past the rhododendron and up towards the house.

The fire had been extensive; the roof had gone and some of the walls had collapsed. Their blackened surfaces had been carpeted over the years by ivy and moss and grass, however, and though from a distance the remaining walls seemed stark and dead, on closer inspection there was a softness about them that was comforting. The sun was warm and the hum of bees in the air gave a pleasant background to his inspection of the ruins. He did not enter them; he suspected they might be dangerously near to collapse, so he contented himself with walking around their perimeter.

His mind drifted back to the Scotswood Road pub where he had met Tiggy Williams; he had thought then of the contrast between the life-styles displayed in the West End of Newcastle and the country seat of Lord Morcomb; now, as he looked at the burned-out ruins of Seddon Burn Hall, he fancied he saw the bridge between them. For one day Sedleigh Hall could look like this, and a way of life that still owed so much to the past might be extinguished. Perhaps by a mundane force such as the Inland Revenue Commissioners, he thought wryly.

He heard the rattle of stone and turned; a moment later he saw her, the big black pacing its nervous way among broken stone, the rider concentrating on the path ahead. She was wearing no riding cap this afternoon, and he realized for the first time that her hair was red-gold in colour, flaming under the warm sun. He moved and her head came up;

she started, dragging on the rein involuntarily in her surprise, and then she recognized him.

'Mr Ward! What are you doing here?' she called, and came towards him.

He glanced back at the ruins. 'Thinking about anachronisms,' he said.

'Is that how you see us?' She was perceptive. And her smile was warm and friendly. She slipped from the saddle and stood looking up at him. He was surprised, again, how small she looked.

'Not exactly anachronistic. But different. Most of the people I know, and have met, live a very different kind of life in very different surroundings from yours.'

Her smile faded and she looked about her. 'But I wonder if they feel different? Oh, superficially, of course they do. But inside, I mean. Me, now, there are times I feel just ... *scared.*'

'Scared of what?'

She looked at him, her eyes wide. 'I'm not certain. The future, I suppose. Daddy's a rich man but when he dies ... it will be mine. That's a responsibility, Mr Ward. Money ... and possessions ... they bring responsibilities that I'm not certain I can match up to.'

'You wouldn't be alone,' Ward said.

She hesitated, not sure what he meant.

'No, probably not. But marriage wouldn't remove the responsibilities. They could be shared, of course, but they'd still be there. And times are changing so rapidly – I sometimes wish I'd been born fifty years earlier. Things were more settled then.'

'Hardly that,' Ward said drily.

She laughed. 'A hundred and fifty, then. But you still haven't explained your presence here. I told you before, I'm the original Nosey Parker.'

'Accident, really. And the same curiosity of character that you suffer from, I suppose. Arthur Egan worked here. I thought I'd like to see ... get the feel of the place.'

She looked about her, frowning. 'I remember it, not well, but vaguely, as it used to be. Now, I ride over here rarely. You ... you're a bit unusual, aren't you, Mr Ward? What's your first name, by the way? I can't keep using these formalities.'

Ward told her and then, as she looped her horse's bridle over a young sycamore that was pushing its way through the base of the wall, he said, 'How do you mean unusual?'

'Coming out here. Going along to Michael's. Do you have a streak of romanticism? I wouldn't have thought in a man–' She was going to say of his age, but caught herself, confused. 'I mean, do solicitors normally poke around old ruins when they administer an estate? Or, I wonder, spend as much time on such a case as you are?'

She was perceptive. And slightly embarrassed. But her embarrassment was now shaded with something else. She was looking at him critically, in a way a woman did not look at a stranger, or a recent acquaintance. 'It's a difficult case,' he said lamely.

'Why?'

He blinked at her directness. 'Well... It's difficult to explain.'

'Difficult case, difficult explanation. So tell me,' she commanded.

Ward smiled, and looked around, leaned against the warm stone wall. The girl followed suit, folding her arms, watching him intently.

And he told her some of it. How he had been a policeman, how he had turned to and been forced towards the solicitor's office, and how he had become involved with the Egan administration. He told her how he felt there was something odd about it all, how the image that had built up in his mind of the lonely man at Westerhope did not square with the picture of a violent struggle on the bridge at Vixen Hill. And he told her about life in the Scotswood Road and in Byker, and about Arthur Egan and his half-brother Tommy, and all the while her eyes never left his face. He was tempted to explain about the other things, Tiggy Williams and Chief Constable Starling, but he held back, for these were matters of rumour perhaps, and bore no real relevance to the search for the beneficiaries to Egan's estate. When he lapsed into silence, she kept that silence for a little while.

'I know what you mean about anachronisms,' she said at last, glancing back over her shoulder at the ruined walls of Seddon Burn Hall. 'What you've told me – it's all so distant from this, and me too, I suppose. Distant in place but in time, too.'

'I'm not really so sure of that. As you said, everyone has responsibilities.'

'Mmmm.' She hesitated. 'Daddy's not too well, you know. It's one of the reasons I came out here today, riding. And why I didn't want David with me. I'm confused...' Again she hesitated. She glanced at him worriedly, as though concerned that she should even be talking like this to a virtual stranger. But she went on. 'You see, David and I ... he wants to marry me and, well, I suppose we have a certain understanding. But I've been in no hurry, and that surely means a certain lack of decisiveness, or something, doesn't it?'

'You're talking of David Penrose.' When she nodded, he said, 'Not necessarily in-decisive. Just ... young.'

He wasn't certain she liked that; she glanced at him sharply and he was again aware of the difference in their respective ages. Then she went on, 'Be that as it may, I'm worried about Daddy, and, I confess, what'll happen if he dies soon. David's there, but...'

'No other close relatives?'

She shook her head and the sunlight glinted on her red-gold hair. 'Not close. There's a branch of the family in Ireland. Daddy hates them; no, loathes them would be a better description. I think it's something to do with the attitudes they displayed during the thirties and forties. Very much a patriot, Daddy couldn't forgive them for some utter-ances they made about Germany. Strange, isn't it, how things said and done in the past can have echoes so many years later?'

'People remember hurts,' Ward said tritely.

She smiled suddenly. 'In fact, as far as I can gather, there must have been quite a performance before Daddy's uncle died. It seems he didn't have quite the same opinion of the Irish branch of the tree as Daddy did, and for a while it was touch and go whether the estates would be willed to him. He was bound to succeed to the title, of course, but as he tells it, there was the chance that much of the trust property would have been put in the way of my Irish relatives. Anyway, the quarrel, or whatever it was, blew over and title and lands came to Daddy. Which really is part of the trouble now.'

'How do you mean?'

'You must remember, Daddy was not a young man when he succeeded to the title. And as soon as he did, this awful business about the estate duty came up. I needn't explain to you just how important it all is – the valuation of the estate is bad enough, but Daddy knows too that even when it's settled he's going to have to find a great deal of ready cash to satisfy the Inland Revenue. It worries him, and he's not well. He can't decide whether to meet the liabilities by sale of some of the land – but he has this idea that he wants the land kept intact for me. I don't really care – though I do care if those horrible open-cast mining people are going to scar the landscape. The alternative is to sell some of his shareholdings. I've talked it over at length with David, and that seems the best solution. The trouble is, if Daddy does sell any of his largest holdings, he will lose quite a lot of money: prices are pretty low and there seems little prospect of them improving in the short term.' She looked at him, smiling again suddenly. 'I sound like a real economist, don't I?'

'In my experience economists aren't as attractive as you.'

'Oh.' It should have been a flippant remark and it should have been received as such. Instead, neither smiled, and she looked away from him. There was a short, edgy silence and Eric Ward cursed himself, wondering what had possessed him to speak as he did, and wondering too why she had reacted the way she did.

After a little while, without looking at him again, and in a reflective tone, she asked, 'Why did you leave the police force? It wasn't just that you'd taken your degree, was it?'

'No.' He hesitated. 'I might have left anyway, but I was told I had glaucoma.'

'Oh.' Again she was silent for a while. 'Did you have treatment ... surgery?'

'No. I keep it at bay.'

There was a stilted quality about the conversation; the earlier confidential ease between them had disappeared. 'Do you miss the police work?' she asked, and it seemed to him a polite, inconsequential, even foolish question.

'It gave me hard work, poor pay, little promotion, much frustration, occasional danger, a broken marriage and, eventually, illness. No, I don't miss police work.'

'I'm sorry.' From the trees on the hill a harsh cawing suddenly broke out as a colony of rooks set up a cacophony, perhaps to drive off an intruder. Anne Morcomb turned her head and looked at Eric Ward. 'You've not thought of marriage again?'

'Once bitten... No, in the police force, it can cause problems. I was away, she was lonely, there was one miscarriage, we saw so little of each other. She found someone else. A common enough story. Absence can sometimes make the heart grow less than fond.'

She smiled faintly. 'Proximity can do the same, I suspect. My mother and father ... they weren't happy, you know. She died when I was quite young, so I don't remember too much about her, except that she was very beautiful, but I do recall the rows they had, and she seemed such a ... sad person, as I remember. I've thought about it as I've grown older and it seems to me to be something I can't understand. You see, it wasn't Daddy's first marriage, and one would think that after one broken marriage a person would take great care in a second choice of partner. Yet I don't think they got on too well. I've talked about it with Michael – you know, Michael Denby. He's older than me, he remembers my mother and he recalls how distant she and Daddy seemed to be. And yet Daddy can be such a loving person. Over the years he's shown me so much overt affection that I wonder why he should, in effect, have failed twice in his marriages.'

'Failure is perhaps overstating it, surely?'

'I don't know. I really don't know.' She rose suddenly, loosened the reins of the black mare and mounted. She sat on the horse, looking down at Eric Ward thoughtfully. 'You haven't told me quite everything about your investigations, have you?'

'I don't know what you mean.'

'Yes you do. In some ways, Eric Ward, you're rather a transparent person. I think you know – or suspect – something about this man Egan that offends ... what? Your sense of justice? And you can't make up your mind what to do about it.'

'As indecisive as you,' he said, smiling.

'You won't put me off with *that* kind of remark,' she replied, but smiled, nevertheless.

'I still feel you know something about Egan that you haven't told me. You also know I'm a very curious person.'

'I agree.'

'So do something about Egan. Don't let it drift. You'll be happier.'

'So might you be,' he replied, and her smile faded. She turned the black's head and began to pace away. When she was some fifty yards off she looked back, but said nothing, then with a touch of her heels she sent the mare galloping towards the trees.

She looked, at this distance, very confident, very sure of herself and her position. But now, Eric Ward knew better.

In a strange way the knowledge depressed him. Over the years he had received many confidences, taken part in many private conversations where people had talked to him of their fears and aspirations and hidden terrors. Little men in darkened rooms, prostitutes drunk in the cells, one arrogant businessman who, under questioning, had suddenly broken down to confess his fraud and expose much, much more of his personality. It happened also in the offices of Francis, Shaw and Elder, with clients who wanted more than merely a legal shoulder to lean on. Legal problems had a way of spilling over into personal ones.

In all these, however, Eric Ward had managed to retain a certain detachment. Express sympathy, but in the main don't feel it: it was too dangerous, and too destructive of logic and reason. Perhaps that was why, now, on a sunny afternoon a conversation with a young woman disturbed and depressed him. She had an inheritance and position – yet she felt indecisive and afraid of the future.

He had no part in that future, and yet his detachment was not complete. He walked back to the car trying to shut thoughts of their conversation out of his mind; her words, and the way she had looked, leaning against the wall of the ruins at Seddon Burn.

In the car he checked the map. It would be necessary to take several minor roads to make his way towards the A1. From there he would need to cut across towards the coast, near Alnwick, and take the run north to Warkworth if he was going to interview Sarah Boden and see the last of the damned Egan administration. He calculated it would take him an hour or more.

In fact it took him longer. The road was more winding than he had expected, and he lost twenty minutes or more behind a herd of cows that were being moved along to a nearby farm. But it was not the time that caused him discomfort. His depression, the driving itself, and the constant reading he had been doing the last few evenings combined to place a tension upon him, physically, that could end in only one way. He knew the attack would come, sooner or later; fortunately, he had reached the A1 before the signals started.

He hesitated briefly about going on to Warkworth, but then decided to do so. It was five o'clock, and he would get some tea in the Northumberland Arms before seeking out Sarah Boden. He did not want to drive up here again tomorrow.

But as he took the road from Felton across towards Warkworth he felt the pain begin. The road twisted and turned, giving him glimpses of the sea while across to his left, beyond the cricket ground, the ruined ramparts of Warkworth Castle reared grandly. He paid them little attention; he concentrated on the road as the feeling of sickness arose in his throat and the tiny needle points of pain began to prick at the back of his eyes, sharp scratchings that grew in intensity and regularity, until he squinted, narrowing his eyes against the pain. He drove down the hill past the castle and swung into Castle Street. He found a parking place down near the church, in the tiny square. He locked his car and with lowered head hurried into the Northumberland Arms. There was an agonized wait of five minutes before the desk clerk was able to give him a room, and then, in the confines of the hotel bedroom he ripped open his briefcase and took out his phial of pilocarpine, applied the fluid to his eyes and waited, lying on the bed, for the shuddering to stop.

He had known the attack would be a bad one. He had known he would not be able to face the drive home afterwards. It was better to wait here, rest, have dinner later and forget office files, Arthur Egan, the Morcomb case and everything else. In the morning he would go to see Sarah Boden, and then go home to change. He should get to the office by ten-thirty.

Now, just relax, rest in the darkened room, and let the drug take effect on his screaming nerve-ends.

Relax, but not entirely, for something fluttered in his mind, unimportant, but demanding his attention, nevertheless. Something about the car parked next to his in the square. Unimportant, especially when matched against the pain in his eyes.

When you were approaching eighty you were entitled to be bloody-minded. You had earned the right and there was no one to gainsay that right. You had worked out your life, and now you had only yourself to please. You had your own house, paid for with your own money earned from generous employers, and you had your own routines. If other people didn't like those routines they could lump it.

And if other people didn't like you not answering the door until you were prepared to do so, they could lump that too.

He knew she was in there, of course. Perversely, when he had started knocking she had made sure that he saw her, moving in the sitting-room, prepared to answer the door only when she wanted to. He was patient, she would say that for him, nevertheless. It was twenty minutes since he had first knocked; he had gone away, then come back again, and now he was still there, knocking. A few more minutes; perhaps five minutes, and then she would answer the door. Perhaps.

It was beginning to get dark. The knocking had stopped. She peered out of the sitting-room window and he was there, just across the street. It was beginning to rain.

When you were eighty, you could get lonely too. She felt sorry for herself, suddenly.

She opened the front door, and stood just inside, in the passageway, where the light fingers of rain could not reach her. He came across after a few moments. He stood in her doorway, smiling at her.

'Hello, Sarah. You do remember me, don't you?'

Chapter Four

1

It rained heavily during the night but by morning the sun was bright again and Ward took an early breakfast, paid his bill and then walked up Castle Street, through the grounds of the castle itself and down the hillside on which it stood. Leaves glistened in the sunlight, still wet from the overnight rain, and the river was at full tide, the small weir virtually submerged, as Ward strolled along the path to talk to the old boatman who made a living hiring rowboats and ferrying across to the far bank those tourists who wished to seek out the Hermit's Cave. He claimed to have been at work there for fifty-eight years, but he still rose early – more for the peace of the river, Ward suspected, than the possibility of hirings.

The walk in the morning sunshine did him a great deal of good. He felt refreshed and his mind was clear. The depression of yesterday was gone. It had probably been induced as much by tiredness as anything else, and the conversation with Anne Morcomb, well, he must be getting fanciful in his old age if he read into it anything other than the obvious – a brief acquaintance, an unhappy time for her, pressures of the kind that for him had resulted in another attack. But this morning things were in perspective, and a blackbird was in full song. Ward turned and followed the stream in its run towards the coast. A few minutes later he had reached the lower end of Warkworth; he paused a while on the ancient bridge watching the house martins under its arches, and then he walked back up the slope of Castle Street.

Enquiries in the shop near the church led to the information that she lived in the first house above the one for sale on the right.

Armed with these directions, Ward found the house easily enough. The house beyond Sarah Boden's seemed to be empty also – Ward suspected some of these granite-fronted houses would be used as second homes by the more affluent on Tyneside.

The door boasted a heavy brass knocker. Ward used it, and listened to the reverberations die away in the house. Surprisingly, the noise had a strangely echoing quality as though the house was empty, but he guessed its structure, or sparse furnishing, would have caused the effect. He tried again and stepped back, almost colliding with a woman walking down the hill with a shopping-bag on her arm. Then again.

There was no answer.

Eric Ward checked his watch. It was just after nine-fifteen. An hour or so home to change; he'd be pushed to get to the office before midday the way things were going. He knocked again, but once more there was no reply. He wondered if she was lying in bed refusing to answer the door. Old people could get like that sometimes; stubborn, peculiar.

He hesitated. There was no sense in waiting any longer, and yet he did not want another journey out to Warkworth from the office. He turned, and walked down the street to the narrow arched alleyway that led to the river bank. These houses had gardens at the rear, overlooking the river. He walked down the alley, then turned to walk along the path that ran through the trees, abutting on the stone wall that enclosed the gardens of the houses in Castle Street.

There were two back gardens tangled with vegetation – one the house for sale, the other, Sarah Boden's. There was no problem in obtaining entry to the garden itself; the wooden door was ajar and when he walked up the pathway through weeds and long grass he saw that the milkman had left a bottle of milk on the back doorstep.

Ward knocked on the back door. The frosted glass prevented his seeing inside but he guessed the kitchen lay beyond. There was no answer. He moved to the window; it was tightly shut apart from its upper section, which was wide open, and gave him a view of the kitchen, in spite of its griminess. He could make out an old gas cooker, linoleum on the floor, a table ... and something else.

It looked like a piece of flowered cloth, lying on the floor.

Had he been a mere solicitor he might have had second thoughts, but years in the police force had trained him otherwise. He went back to the frosted glass door and shattered it with his elbow. He punched out the glass, cutting his hand in the process, then gingerly inserted his hand and opened the door.

She was lying on her back in her flowered dress. There was a cut on her forehead and her eyes were wide open, staring. The hissing noise came from the open gas tap on the cooker. Ward reached down and lightly took her wrist. There was no pulse. He went back out into the fresh morning air. He would have to phone for an ambulance, but he knew that he was already too late.

It did not take as long as he had anticipated. He placed calls to the ambulance service and to the police, then rang his office to explain he would not be in today. Then he waited. They all arrived within a few minutes of each other; ambulance, squad car, uniformed local policeman. They questioned him, looked sour when he told them he knew nothing regarding the circumstances of death, and sourer when they saw the broken door. Then the doctor arrived to pronounce Sarah Boden dead. Ward was asked to accompany the squad car in his own vehicle to Morpeth; there he was questioned and made a statement.

It was over.

But finished in more ways than one. Eric Ward doubted whether Jackie Parton would now discover very much more, if anything, about the remote Arthur Egan, and with the death of Sarah Boden it was unlikely that he himself would find out anything that might help in the administration of the estate.

No relatives; the last fantasies of a dying man, creating a family where none existed.

He was back at his office early next morning, to make up for lost time.

At eleven o'clock Joseph Francis rang through to ask Eric to join him for coffee. It was an unusual summons, for the senior partner confined business meetings to the afternoon and social meetings to the early evenings. During the mornings he worked at his own files, the habit of a lifetime in the law.

But there the coffee was, in two delicate china cups, and Joseph Francis waved Eric to the leather armchair. It was unlikely that the occasion was destined to be a social one, however, for Joseph's face was serious, and his mouth pursed. He stared at Eric Ward with a hint of belligerence.

'What do you really think of my son Paul?' he asked abruptly.

Ward made no reply immediately. He stared at the older man, frowning. 'In what respect do you mean?'

'Don't be so damned coy. You know what I mean.'

The testiness in Francis's tone annoyed Ward. 'I don't know what you mean. Socially? I can answer that easily enough. But professionally? I don't think that's the kind of question a senior partner should ask an articled clerk.'

'You're not exactly the usual kind of articled clerk,' Francis snapped. 'I wouldn't go around asking a twenty year old such a question. I'm asking you because I want your professional opinion of him.' He paused, then added grudgingly, 'And because I – value your opinion, as well.'

This, Ward thought, could very well be where he and Francis, Shaw and Elder parted company, but if Joseph really wanted his opinion, he could have it, for not to give it now would somehow damage his own independence and pride. 'All right, sir, I'll tell you. I think he's competent, but not sufficiently prepared to undertake the hard grind. I suspect he has flair, but he exercises it on matters that are of interest to him only. I've seen him in litigation and he can be sharp, and quick. In the office, he's not like that. I think he needs a challenge; I think he needs incentive. He's easily bored, and when that happens he doesn't work well.'

'You don't think much of Paul then?' Joseph Francis sneered.

Aware that the old man would be feeling the criticism personally, Ward replied, 'You asked for my opinion. I believe I stressed what Paul's better points might be also, professionally speaking.'

'Hmmm.' Joseph Francis raised a hand and touched his hair, as though checking that its silvery neatness was as precise as ever. When he spoke again, his tone was back to its normal, slightly bored modulation. 'Well, you may well be right, of course. Er ... how long have you got to complete your articles?'

'Just over eight months.'

'And then what?'

As Joseph Francis reached out an elegant hand to pick up his coffee cup Ward hesitated. 'I'm not sure, sir. An assistant solicitor post somewhere, I suppose.'

'Here?'

'I think that's for you and the other partners to say.'

Francis sipped his coffee, made a slight

grimace at its apparent bitterness, then looked carefully at Ward. 'Eight months, hey? All right, I'll tell you what, Eric. No promises, but there may be a place for you here. As an assistant – but with prospects. Maybe, two years, and the chance to buy in as a junior partner. No promises – and it depends on your exams, of course, and on your performance. You see, there may be a position...'

'I'd be grateful for the opportunity.'

Joseph Francis looked at him with cold eyes. 'It's partly because of Paul. He hasn't made up his mind yet, but you're right in your assessment. I've already spoken to him; I'll finance him if he'd like to go to the bar, where he could utilize his forensic talents more adequately.' His tone was dry. 'So if he goes, there could well be a place for you. The devil we know and all that. Just one trouble, on the other hand...'

Ward held his glance. 'Yes?'

'Balance. A sense of balance is necessary to a solicitor. And a low profile. Very necessary.'

'I don't quite understand what you're getting at,' Ward lied.

'Time is money,' Francis said flatly. 'Some of the drudgery that suits Paul so ill brings us in our largest profits. We need to concentrate

160

on such matters. Estate administration – unless of the largest kind – is not very profitable. One should not allow unproductive work to push aside bread-and-butter files. It's time you finished that damned Egan business: you're spending too much time on it.'

'You also said something about a low profile.'

Joseph Francis sipped his coffee. 'Clients must respect their solicitor. They must have confidence in him, hold his judgement in high regard. Scandal of any kind drives away clients, prospective and actual. Conduct in any way ... *outré* has the same effect. Now then – what exactly went on yesterday?'

Ward took a deep breath. 'I went to interview a woman. When I arrived I found she was dead. I broke into the house, then called the necessary services. I made a statement to the police, then went home.'

'How did she die?'

'I think she must have gone to the kitchen to make some tea or something, turned on the gas, then slipped on the linoleum and knocked herself out. She was there all night; it might have been the cold; there was no heat in the kitchen, and the window was open; it could have been pneumonia. She was pretty old.'

Joseph Francis was only slightly mollified. 'An accident,' he murmured, then sipped again at his coffee. 'All right, Eric, but remember what I said. Housebreaking is for burglars; dead people are for undertakers. You're neither.'

'Necessity–'

'–is the mother of convention, Eric!' Joseph Francis interrupted swiftly. 'Remember that. You need a job with us; in our own way, we need you. But convention demands that solicitors behave like solicitors – discreet, controlled, genteel if you like. In America things may be different, but over here we have a set of values that have been proved over a hundred years.' He leaned back, a frown gathering on his patrician features, nettled somewhat that his little speech had bordered on the excited. 'Let's say no more about it, Eric. Just remember what I've told you.'

Ward rose to his feet, and began to walk to the door.

Francis stopped him. 'Before you go, I should tell you that counsel's opinion on Lord Morcomb's case is expected tomorrow. I'll let you have it once I've finished with it. That case could be ... very helpful to you, Eric, if we do a good job on it. And otherwise, just one more thing.'

'Yes, sir?'

'I want the Egan administration dispensed with. This week.'

2

Back in his own room Eric did not know whether to feel elated or depressed. The knowledge that Paul Francis could well be leaving the firm, with a consequent assistant post being available, and even a partnership, was exciting: it meant that if he pulled his weight during the next eight months and completed the papers that remained to him of the Law Society examinations, he could be obtaining a secure future for himself in a leading law firm in Newcastle. Yet at the same time, in spite of the prospect opening up ahead of him, he felt edgy and ill at ease, with the sense of something unfinished remaining. Anne Morcomb had told him to complete the Egan enquiry, but would it ever end? And for that matter, was it not already ended, with the accidental death of Sarah Boden?

This week, Joseph Francis had warned; it had to be finished this week. As far as Eric Ward was concerned, it would be as well if it finished right now. The file was on his desk; he closed it, placing it in the filing cabinet. A few days more and if there were no replies to the advertisements he'd go ahead with the payment of debts and other outgoings and then get the estate declared *bona vacantia*.

He was done with Arthur Egan. He had his own career to look to.

The following morning he received a visitor who showed him that the file was far from closed.

The secretary showed him in and withdrew but her leaving did little to empty the room because Detective Chief Superintendent Arkwright had the presence and the bulk to make any room look small. He was six feet two in his stockinged feet and had long ago put behind him the youthful awkwardness of a raw Yorkshire recruit. Once away from the uniformed branch he had begun to 'put on weight, and good living had thickened his waist, deepened his chest as he combined regular exercise with heavy meals. For a period he had been a weightlifting champion in police circles and he had used the same commitment to the pursuit of his ambition. It was now more or less achieved: further promotion was possible, but not likely, and he was generally satisfied with his job. Traces of his Yorkshire background remained in his speech, and his ruddy complexion, craggy nose and mouth were those that would have fitted a hill farmer in the dales. He occasionally pretended a simplicity that he had lost over the years, but Eric Ward knew him to be a confident and resourceful jack.

'Well, well, lad, tha's done well enough, hey? Nice little room, nice little secretary, the quiet easy life, is that it?' He moved forward, light on his feet for such a big man and settled himself in a chair facing Ward. 'Any chance of a coffee, then?'

Ward picked up the phone and dialled reception. 'This a social call? Er ... can you send up two coffees as soon as possible?' He replaced the phone and looked at Arkwright. 'Or is it in the way of business?'

Arkwright smiled benignly and pulled at his ear. 'Bit of both, really. Thought it'd be nice to see how you're getting on, now you've crossed to t'other side.'

'Not exactly the other side, surely.'

'Well, you know how I mean.' Arkwright grinned.

'How's your eyes, anyway?'

'I'm well enough.'

'Loss to the Force, Eric, loss to the Force.'

Ward made no reply; Arkwright had been conspicuous in expressing no sympathy at the time of Ward's departure. He listened as Arkwright wandered on, talking about some of his ex-colleagues, bringing him up to date on movements. They had been surprisingly numerous, even though Ward had been away for only eighteen months. The secretary came in with the coffees and Arkwright thanked her graciously. When she'd gone he picked up his cup and quite deliberately sipped it with noisy gusto. 'No, you seem to have settled in nicely enough, Eric, you have that.'

'I don't think you've really called to comment upon the degree of comfort I enjoy.'

'No need to get acid, Eric.' Arkwright's words were placatory but there was an edge of steel in his voice. 'If you must know, I just called to discuss with you how you seemed to be doing some funny things, beyond the call of a solicitor's duty, like.'

'Yes?' Ward said unhelpfully.

'Yes. Like breaking and entering, for instance,' Arkwright said affably. 'Not usually in a solicitor's line of work.'

Ward recalled Joseph Francis's words and his mouth was tight. 'I realized something was wrong in Sarah Boden's house. When I broke in, I discovered she was dead. My being a solicitor had nothing to do with it.'

'Mmm. No, suppose not. You – er – you stayed over in Warkworth evening before, didn't you?' Arkwright's eyes fixed on him over the rim of the coffee cup. 'Did you go up to see her then?'

Ward shook his head. 'I intended to. I – I didn't feel well enough, so I booked a room in the hotel and ate there, rested, went to see her next morning.'

'What did you want to see her about, then?' The tone was still casual, but Ward was gaining the impression that there was something more important behind this visit than he realized.

'I'm dealing with an administration matter. I thought she might be able to give me some information – local gossip if you like, that she might have picked up twenty years ago–'

'Twenty years?'

'–when she was working at a house in Northumberland which has since burned down. It was a slim chance and now it's too late anyway... Just what is this all about, Arkwright?'

The big man shook his head slowly. 'Come to that in a moment. First of all, I know you gave a statement, but like to tell me about it again? You know the form – in case you ... er ... missed anything at the time.'

Ward suppressed an angry reply and patiently went over what he had already said to the police at Morpeth. Arkwright asked him a few questions about the position of the body, and the state of the kitchen when he entered it, then asked him if he had entered any other part of the house. When he denied doing so, Arkwright frowned. 'Mmmm. And you didn't move the body?'

'Couldn't be sure she was dead. I just left, and called the ambulance and the police.'

'Mmm. Interesting.'

Ward regarded him stonily for a short while. Then he said, 'You'd better tell me.'

Arkwright finished his coffee and put the cup down with a clatter. 'Not a lot to tell you, really. Just questions to ask. In case.'

'In case of what?'

'In case the labs at Gosforth come up with the kind of report the liaison officer there tells me they might produce. You see, they're a bit puzzled, down there in Gosforth.'

'What about?'

'The old lady, she goes into the kitchen just when it's getting dark, to make a cup of tea, maybe, on the gas. Maybe she's looking for the matches, and she turns, and maybe slips

168

on the lino. She bangs her head – not a bad blow, but she's eighty, after all, and maybe the sudden shock, the surprise, the fall, it knocks her out for a while. And she lies there while the rain comes down and the kitchen is cold and the window open. Cold night air, thin dress ... and a weak old lady...' He leaned back in his chair, squinted thoughtfully at Eric Ward. 'She *was* dead when you found her?'

'I'm certain of it.'

'Touch her?'

'Just her pulse.'

Arkwright bared his teeth in a grimace. 'Wonder what made the scratches on her neck, then?'

The room was still for a moment. 'Scratches?' Ward repeated stupidly.

'Scratches,' Arkwright repeated emphatically. 'Made before death. No cats in the house. Maybe something under her own nails, but I doubt it. Bit of bruising too, hip, upper arms. All before death, you see, but not long before. And you say you didn't go around there the night before?'

'No.'

'Funny.' Arkwright stared at him thoughtfully. 'You see, there's a woman lives up above this Boden woman who says she saw someone knocking at the door in the rain the previous evening. Then, next morning, she's going down to do her shopping and there's a feller standing knocking again – almost collides with him as he stepped back. She *thinks* it was the same man.'

'She's wrong,' Ward said flatly. 'I remember colliding with some woman that morning – but I wasn't there the night before.'

'No. If you say so.' Arkwright considered the matter for a few moments. 'So you wouldn't have draped a wet raincoat over the banisters of the stairs either, so it made a puddle on the carpet?'

Ward made no reply; he had already stated the truth. 'You don't think her death was an accident,' he said slowly.

'Oh, I didn't say that. We've got to wait for the lab report from Gosforth. But let's say my experienced nose detects something malodorous.' He placed his hands on the arms of his chair, preparatory to rising. 'All right, that'll do for now. But you're sure there's nothing more, you can tell me?'

Ward shook his head and Arkwright grimaced, then heaved himself to his feet, glanced around him once more to smile an insincerely appreciative smile and turned to leave.

'There is one thing,' Ward said as Arkwright was about to open the door.

'Yeh?'

'You haven't asked me for details about why I wanted to see her.'

Arkwright raised his eyebrows mockingly. 'You told me you were doing something about the administration of an estate. But lawyers are close-mouthed about their clients' affairs. I didn't expect you'd answer me if I asked for details.'

'This client is dead.'

Arkwright considered the matter. 'There'll be beneficiaries – don't you really act for them as well?'

'I can't find them. That's why I was going to question Sarah Boden.'

Arkwright grinned unpleasantly. 'We all got our problems. You – a dead client, and a dead … what would you call her? Witness?' He shrugged. 'So tell me your problem.'

'Not exactly a problem.'

'So what, then?'

'The dead client was Arthur Egan.'

If he had expected an immediate reaction, Eric Ward was disappointed. Arkwright stared at him expectantly for a moment as though assuming he had more to say. Then his mouth twisted slightly, as though he was about to make a sneering, dismissive remark to suggest the name meant nothing to him. It was several seconds before Ward saw the slow seeping of memory darken Arkwright's eyes, and then the big man stood there staring at Ward, but not seeing him, as his memory cells produced facts and faces and names. 'Arthur Egan,' he said at last, but with a hint of defensiveness and caution. 'Can't say it rings any bells for me, exactly.'

'Then I'll ring a couple for you,' Ward said quietly. 'Just over twenty years ago he was charged with murder. He copped manslaughter and served seven years.'

'There's a few of them about. I don't–'

'When he got out he lived quietly in Westerhope, and died recently. But since I started dealing with his estate I've been hearing some funny things.'

'You have, hey?' Arkwright stood squarely, facing him. 'And no doubt you're going to tell me about them.'

'That's right. Because I'm beginning to think Egan was railroaded.'

Arkwright had control of his eyes now; he stared without expression at Ward. 'Just what is that supposed to mean?' he asked calmly.

'Egan may well have been guilty of the crime – the killing of Colonel Denby – but it begins to look to me as though the evidence was planted to make sure a conviction was brought in.'

There was a short silence, as Arkwright continued to stare impassively at Eric Ward. 'Just why are you telling me all this?'

'Because the way I hear it, you were responsible for the planting of some of that evidence. Wittingly or unwittingly, you helped put Egan away for seven years!'

A flush now stained Arkwright's heavy face. He came back two steps towards Ward's desk, threateningly. 'You just better watch your mouth, Ward. That kind of talk can get a man into trouble!'

'Not if he can prove what he says!' Ward was trembling.

He had no idea now why he was talking this way to Arkwright; perhaps it had been the result of the man's attitude when he entered the room; perhaps it was merely that Arkwright was the catalyst for all the doubts and pressures that had been stirring in Ward's mind since he had first become involved with the Egan administration.

Arkwright thrust his head forward. His tone was ugly. 'Listen to me, friend. It seems to me you're a bit off track. I don't know what the hell's got into you, but this rubbish you're spouting – hell, you're talking about a prosecution twenty years old! The man himself is dead! What's the point of stirring things up now – did *he* ever do it, when he got out? What makes you the great saviour of reputations? Egan was guilty; he served his time; then he tried to forget about it. You ought to do the same.'

'And what if he *wasn't* guilty?'

The words lay in the air between them like an obscenity. Arkwright was glaring at him, his face purpling, his big hands at his sides, clenched as though he was restraining himself only with the greatest difficulty. At last he said, 'I'm going to forget this rubbish you're saying, Ward. Because it would be unproductive to do anything about it. I got a job to do over this Sarah Boden business – and it's got nothing to do with a twenty year old manslaughter case. Now if you got anything to say to help over the Boden death, all right. If not – keep your mouth shut.' He turned away, angrily, making for the door again. He opened it, then paused, looked back and said in an even tone, 'Remember this, too. Push things...' He hesitated, and again Ward got the impression that he was thinking back, combing through his memory for half-forgotten truths. 'Push things ... and you might find yourself facing guns big enough to blow you to little pieces!'

He left, and Ward heard him stamping angrily down the stairs. Anger still stirred Eric Ward's blood and he could hardly think straight as a result. He cursed himself for being so direct with Arkwright: if he had played him more gently he might have discovered more about the Egan case of twenty years ago from the man who had been a constable on the case.

It was only when he had calmed down that he realized Arkwright had not denied that evidence had been planted against Arthur Egan.

3

Jackie Parton slipped out of the pub to meet Ward as arranged. Eric Ward had had enough of public houses with their smoke-filled atmospheres; he wanted to talk to Parton but he wanted to walk, too, in the fresh air. He had worked doggedly all afternoon on the Morcomb files again and he was tired, but the Egan case still haunted him – and haunted was the word. He wanted desperately to have done with it suddenly; he had instructions from Joseph Francis to complete

175

the administration, and he wanted Egan off his mind. But it would not be possible while anger stirred in his veins, against Arkwright, against the people behind Arkwright who might have pressurized Tiggy Williams and others to send Egan to prison.

'This is a pretty sudden assumption you're making,' Jackie Parton said carefully, as they walked along the Quayside and under the span of the Tyne Bridge shadowing the dark evening water.

'That maybe Arthur Egan wasn't guilty?' Ward shook his head desperately. 'I don't know ... there's just something odd about the whole case. Look, Egan was a quiet, reserved person as a lad – isn't that the picture you've got of him? Quiet, and responsible. He goes off to the country when his mother settles into a new marriage – but he still comes back to see his half-brother. And then, suddenly, he takes to burglary, for God's sake! And more – he clubs down a man and kills him, when threatened with a shotgun! It's not in character. Not the character of the man I seem to see.'

Parton was silent for a while. Traffic roared over the bridge behind and above them; the dark outline of a naval vessel berthed at the Gateshead side lay solid against the slope of the river banks. 'All right, you'd better go on, if you go that far.'

'I don't know that I can! There are other ... odd situations, but they don't seem to make sense, don't seem to tie in to the burglary at Vixen Hill. To start with, why the hell did Egan go back there, when he had been released from prison? Remorse ... curiosity? It's such an odd thing to do. And Fred Bridges – I just don't believe him when he says he fixed that job for Egan because he liked him. He held something back from me, I'm sure of it. But what – and why?'

Jackie Parton sloughed along beside him, hands in pockets, his shadow squat and foreshortened as they passed under the lights of the freighter moored at the Quayside. 'Well, then, let's go back a bit and take a different angle to what you've been saying. You know, there's one feller in all this who stays kind of shady, you know? We've got some bloody photographs of him, but he's just not around to answer questions.'

'You mean the half-brother – Tommy Andrews?'

Jackie Parton nodded and fingered his scarred lip.

'Egan still kept hold of those photographs. All his life. For my book, I reckon that means he thought a hell of a lot of his kid brother ... or half-brother ... makes no difference, really. I wonder just how much he *did* think of him? How much he would do for him?'

Ward glanced thoughtfully at the ex-jockey. 'He kept going back to see him, as a youngster, until he went to sea.'

'Yeh. Until he went to sea. But you know, in old people's minds things get telescoped, sometimes. What if the timing of things are a bit different? I was told by Granny Skipton that Andrews went to sea, so Egan never came back to Byker no more – and of course, the old woman then said she knew nothing about Egan's "trouble".'

He snickered softly. 'The sequence could have been a little bit different.'

'In what way?'

'You talked about Egan's character – the way you see him. I don't disagree too much – take away the Colonel Denby killing and the seven years inside and what have we got? A citizen, that's all – a quiet, reserved feller, kind of sad and lonely, I reckon. Maybe missing his brother?'

'That's about it.'

'But let's take a look at Tommy Andrews. By all accounts a young tearaway. In scrapes as a kid – and I've picked up a couple of hints that he was hauled up a couple of times. Now he was in no way destined to be a model citizen. Would we be surprised if he had decided to turn his hand to a bit of burglary?'

'Are you suggesting–'

'Look, we know that Egan took Andrews out to the country with him at one time, but Tommy didn't like it – preferred the city,' Parton said with a hint of excitement in his voice. 'And we know he was a bit of a wild lad, too. Now what if he took it in his head one night to do the place at Vixen Hill? He could have seen it, passed it, looked it over while he was out with Egan. What if he'd gone to stay with Egan – and then tried it on at Vixen Hill? Or even just gone out there from town – it was common knowledge Colonel Denby kept a silver collection in the farm. Bloody fool: half the thieves in Newcastle would have hungered for it but wouldn't have been stupid enough to try a *colonel* – and they were right, with *that* shotgun-happy bastard! But a wild kid like Tommy Andrews... So tell me this, Eric. What would big brother Egan do if the kid came runnin' out of the night with blood on his clothes, begging Arthur to do what he always did – get him out of trouble?'

Ward stopped, and turned to stare at the little man beside him. 'His instinct would be to help him out of the mess – at least, unless he knew Tommy had killed someone.'

'Would Tommy tell him – even if he was certain?' Ward nodded thoughtfully. 'A change of clothing, a warning to get out of the district, and Egan ... Egan would take it on himself to destroy the clothing–'

'Especially if, after Tommy had skedaddled and was heading for Liverpool or God's to know where, the news came that Colonel Denby had croaked it.'

'But when the police tracked to Egan's cottage, and it came out from the – the–'

'The Salter woman.'

'–that she'd seen him burning blood-stained clothing, he would surely have–'

'Uh-uh!' Jackie Parton held up his hand, gave a knowing shake of his head. 'Think back, lad. Arthur Egan is innocent – okay, accomplice after the fact maybe, but he didn't croak Denby. He *knows* he's innocent. Maybe he's got a naive belief in British justice, who knows? But more important – if the police come questioning him is he going to shop the kid? The hell he is!'

Eric Ward nodded. He tried to think of the way the young Arthur Egan would have reacted; the prison years would have changed him, but not enough to make him throwaway the photographs of his young half-brother. And later, when the other evidence comes up it's too late.'

'He could have fought harder,' Parton agreed. 'But the daft bastard was still protecting his brother. And *he'd* scooted, off to sea and a life rolling from port to port. Or...'

They had reached the end of the Quayside; Parton lit a cigarette and drew on it, his features caricatured in the glow of the cigarette. 'It still is a bit hard to believe, his taking the sentence to save Andrews, who had gone off to sea. It'd make more sense if Andrews never did go off to the rolling wave.'

'How do you mean?' Ward asked.

'What if he stayed in the country? Just dropped out of sight – left Tyneside? For that matter, maybe he didn't even leave Tyneside – just got away from Byker, like Egan did. Close community, around the Wall, but they don't know a damn thing about Egan after he left – except for the conviction. If Tommy'd left – they wouldn't know much about him, either. Big place, Tyneside. He could've gone to Shields, Sunderland... If he was still around, what could Egan do except take the medicine handed out to him?'

The more Ward thought about it, the more convinced he became that Parton was right. He had not consciously allowed it to come as a possibility to the front of his own mind, and yet how else could he explain his outburst to Arkwright, and his dogged, obsessional commitment to the case? He had shouted at Arkwright – 'What if he wasn't guilty?' The thought had been there at the back of his mind, in the recesses of his subconscious – it was Parton who was now giving logical foundations to what had been a suspicion.

And if Tommy Andrews had not gone to sea ... if Tommy Andrews were still alive, on Tyneside...

'All theorizin', of course,' Parton said carelessly, as they turned to retrace their steps along the quay. 'And all a bit pointless, really. Egan's dead ... what's there to prove?' What indeed – especially when it was all irrelevant to the purpose of Ward's initial enquiries. 'It still leaves some unanswered questions, nevertheless,' Ward said.

'Like Vixen Hill,' Parton suggested.

'That's right. Something there drew Egan back. But if it was Tommy Andrews who went there and killed Denby, what was its fascination for Egan? And there's another thing, too.'

'Yeh?'

Something crossed his mind momentarily, a dark image he could not grasp. He shook his head. 'Detective Chief Superintendent Arkwright came to see me today. He got somewhat annoyed when I raised the matter of the planting of evidence in the Egan case twenty years ago.'

'Understandable,' Parton grinned, in the darkness. 'Done well, has that lad. But he can be a bad enemy.'

'The thing is, he came to see me about the body I discovered at Warkworth.'

'Hell's flames!' Parton stopped, stared at him in surprise. 'No bugger tells me anything around here! Who the hell—'

'She was called Sarah Boden. I intended asking her some questions about the possibility of Arthur Egan having fathered a child on one of the local dairymaids or stable girls. But when I got there, she was dead.'

'And Arkwright—'

'Detective Chief Superintendent Arkwright wasn't exactly saying so, but he hinted that the death might not have been natural.'

They said nothing more until they reached

Dog Leap Stairs. Parton looked up at him and said quietly, 'You ... er ... you're suggesting that maybe there's some connection between what we been saying and this woman's death?'

'I don't know. It... I can't see any link yet. Maybe there is none. But for a couple or more days I'd just like to see what we can find out – and to hell with the Francises and the Arkwrights of this world. There's an answer somewhere, if we can find it ... Tommy Andrews ... that photograph of the grave ... Sarah Boden maybe, too. And...'

The image was before his mind again, dark, crumpled.

He seized it, held it. 'And there's one thing more you can do, Jackie.'

'Yeh?'

'Get up to Warkworth; make some enquiries. When I parked in the square, the car next to mine was one I'd seen before. It was a black Ford with a crumpled wing. I can remember the driver – youngish, fair hair. But I'd seen the car before.' He paused, thinking. 'Check the hotels in Warkworth. You might get hold of the registration, and trace the owner–'

'*If* he stayed in any of them hotels,' Parton grumbled. 'Where had you seen this car before, anyway?'

'Just the once. When I was driving down a narrow lane – on the way from Sedleigh Hall to Vixen Hill.'

Chapter Five

1

The forensic laboratories in Gosforth were situated in a series of single-storey brick buildings linked by connecting passageways that always reminded Eric Ward of rabbit runs. He had undertaken a spell as liaison officer with the forensic scientists when he had been newly promoted to Detective Inspector and he knew both the buildings and the people who worked there well. During that period he had learned of the curious hostility that the scientists could bring to bear against the police; it was as though they suspected constantly that their skills and knowledge might be the subject of manipulation, that they might be trapped into making statements that had no real basis of dispassionate, scientific truth, and consequently, until they felt they could trust the officers with whom they dealt their manner could be distinctly cool. It had been Ward's first task to break down that thinly veiled hostility.

Now, some years later, he was not certain what kind of reception he might get. He was no longer in the police force, and he had no official business there. At least he had no problem getting in; during his time there security had been pretty tight with passes having to be shown at the entrances, but it was obvious now that the scares of recent years had settled down, and the Civil Service no longer seemed to suspect an IRA man behind every charming smile.

In fact, he need not have worried about his reception. He made his way to the laboratories and asked a white-coated girl where he might find Gus Thomas. He was relieved to hear that Gus still had his old office, tucked away in a corner from the main working laboratories – relieved, because he had never become accustomed to viewing with equanimity some of the work and some of the specimens displayed at the laboratories. And when he tapped on Gus Thomas's door and was invited to enter, the look on the civil servant's face warmed him.

'Eric! How nice to see you again! Come in, come in, and I'll get you a cup of tea!'

The little grey-haired man with the striped shirt, polka-dotted bow tie and shabby grey suit waved him to a chair, produced two grimy tea cups and a half-bottle of Scotch, and proceeded to pour two generous measures of whisky. Eric Ward held up a warning hand. 'Sorry, Gus, not for me. Warned off.'

Gus Thomas stared at him for a moment with a professional air, as though looking for the signs around Eric's eyelids, and then he nodded, looked at one of the cups and pulled a face. 'Can't go sticking that back in the bottle; sacrilege.' He drank it down with a flourish and another grimace, contemplated the second cup and then reluctantly placed it on top of the filing cabinet behind him. Eric suspected it would not stay there very long.

Their talk consisted of pleasantries for a little while, with Gus rambling on about the period Eric had spent as liaison officer and the occasional binge they had had in a local pub in Gosforth High Street, but at last he asked Eric directly what had brought him to the laboratories.

'Fishing, really,' Eric said.

'For facts.'

'That's right.'

'As opposed to fiction,' Gus Thomas said contemptuously. 'That's what really gets up my nose, Eric, and always has done. Too many coppers come in here knowing exactly what happened – or what they *think* happened – at a scene of crime, and expect us to produce scientific evidence of the occurrences. And if we come up with facts that show the events didn't happen or couldn't have happened, hell, it's not just they don't want to know, they actually yell that we're perverting the course of justice!'

'I know what you mean.'

'And then there's the other kind who come stamping in expecting us to provide *answers*, not just facts. Hell, all we can do is say what we find, not how or why it got there. Still...' Gus Thomas broke off, watching Eric thoughtfully for a moment. 'Facts, you said. You're not in the police any more. You investigating something and want some good professional advice, hey?'

'Not exactly.' Eric hesitated. 'I really wanted to get some information about a job you're looking at right now. A police matter.'

Gus Thomas frowned. His eyes drifted to the cup of Scotch on the filing cabinet, and then back to Eric again. 'Tricky.'

'I realize that – and I accept you might not

feel able to tell me very much, if anything.'

'What's the case?'

'An old lady. Sarah Boden.'

Gus Thomas nodded. 'We got her down in the lab. Interesting case... And I've had that bloody slob Arkwright on my back already. Why the hell he can't leave things to his liaison man ... you were a good liaison copper, Eric.' His glance drifted to the cup of whisky again. 'Oh, what the hell!' He reached back, took down the cup and sipped at the whisky appreciatively. It mellowed his judgement. 'All right, ask away, Eric, and if I can help, I will.'

'I found the body, Gus. I thought it was an accident. But I've seen Arkwright too, and he dropped a few hints which lead me to believe it wasn't an accident. I want no more than that, really – to know what you've found to suggest one thing or the other.'

'If that's all you want to know, there's no real problem – because I know I can trust your discretion. But a straight answer ... well, that's not so easy.'

'How do you mean?'

'Let me put it like this. That old lady, she had a visitor, right? If she hadn't, she'd still be alive. But whether it was a deliberate killing ... that'd be difficult to prove.'

Eric Ward was puzzled. 'What have you got, then?'

'Not a great deal,' Gus Thomas admitted. 'Some scratches on her neck; bruises on the upper arms and the thigh, left side. Contusions of a minor nature elsewhere; the scalp wound; a displaced vertebra, not much more than that.'

'Cause of death?'

Thomas sniffed and sipped his whisky. 'Couldn't have been any heat in the kitchen. Hypothermia ... but maybe shock. Difficult to say how long she's been dead, you see.'

Eric Ward was silent for a little while. The forensic scientist watched him, and waited. He knew what was coming. 'It'll only be an educated guess,' he said softly, 'and I wouldn't do it for Arkwright, because he'd try to make it official. But for you...'

'All right, tell me what you think happened, Gus.'

Gus Thomas nodded, satisfied. Much as he might complain about the questions police officers asked him, and much though he might deny he produced anything other than facts from evidence supplied him, he nevertheless loved – with the right people – to discuss hypothetical possibilities. This was one of those times. 'I wouldn't know how long her visitor was in the house, but it wasn't long. I did a scale on the temperature, speed of drying, amount of water on the carpet – and I guess he wasn't there more than an hour.'

'He?'

'Can't be positive, but some of the fluff picked off her clothes suggests contact with male suiting. But not easy... Anyway, he wasn't there long – and maybe he didn't intend to kill her, and maybe it was all pretty botched anyway. My hypothesis would be that he got niggled with her, perhaps took her by her upper arms and shook her, pretty violently. It displaced a small bone in her neck, and she was in pain. She might even have fainted. And then, or maybe earlier, this character also got his hands on her neck – maybe in the same argument. Then, when she was unconscious he dragged her into the kitchen – there are marks in the hallway, and carpet threads in her shoes – dropped her and left her there for the cold to deal with.'

'What about the wound on her head?'

'*Could* have been enough to stun her, but I doubt it. Shock could have done it, of course – but I suspect she maybe fainted when he was shaking her. But it was all a bit botched, and amateurish.'

'How do you mean?' Eric asked.

Gus Thomas finished the whisky, and gazed reluctantly at the empty cup. 'Come on, Eric, if you were going to knock off a frail old lady wouldn't you make the scene a bit more convincing? And leaving her in the cold kitchen, for God's sake! That was taking a chance. She might have come around, crawled to the door. Unless she'd already stopped breathing – which is possible. No ... he took chances, a real amateur job.'

'Effective enough, nevertheless.'

Gus Thomas grimaced. 'Admit that. But untidy. I will say one thing, though. He's a cool bastard. He shook hell out of that old girl and when she dropped on him he decided to kill her. He took her in the kitchen and deliberately banged her head, hard, against the cooker. Takes a peculiar kind of savagery to do that, you know, to an unconscious old woman. Oh, aye, a cool bastard.'

'And that's what you think happened?' Eric asked. 'That's what I think happened. But I'd never swear to it in a court of law. All I'd point to would be the facts – and for a fact, this bloody cup is empty. You staying long, Eric?'

Eric wasn't staying long.

He had another call to make in Gosforth – the witnessing of a will, which he had used as an excuse at the office to come out in the direction of the forensic laboratories – and when that task was completed he made his way back to Francis, Shaw and Elder in a thoughtful mood. To date, his basic intention had been to discover the beneficiaries, if any, of the Egan estate. Last evening, with Jackie Parton, he had decided to finish the other task with which he had become obsessed – the discovery of the truth about Egan and Colonel Denby, and the possible rehabilitation of Egan's name. But it had all been an exercise in the past, a dredging of old waters. Now suddenly there was the distinct possibility that the past had come alive and was very much part of the present. It was a sobering thought. Arkwright's hints had been one thing; Gus Thomas's hypothesis had been another. He had trust in the judgement of the little man in Gosforth. He was too experienced a scientist to be far wrong in his deductions.

When he entered the office the receptionist signalled to him. He stuck his head around the door and she told him, somewhat flustered by a call coming in, that there was a client waiting for him in his room.

Ward frowned. He wasn't expecting anyone, and he was not really in the mood for an interview almost before he had got back to his room. No doubt it would be someone Paul had foisted off on him. He walked quickly up the stairs and entered his room.

The woman rose from the chair to face him. It was Anne Morcomb.

She was dressed in a dark blue suit that showed off her figure to considerable advantage but her manner was restrained, slightly nervous, as though she felt ill at ease in this room. He went forward to shake her hand, but her smile was faint, and tremulous at the edges. She sat down as he walked behind his desk; he felt as nervous as she looked.

'I'm surprised to see you here,' he said inanely. 'You look ... different.'

'I could hardly visit town in jodhpurs,' she said, but the smile slipped again and she looked intensely at him, with a frown creasing her forehead. 'I heard this morning ... about Sarah.'

So that was it. Eric Ward sat down and contemplated his hands for a few moments. His nervousness was dying, to be replaced by something else – a slight anxiety. This girl was going to ask questions; he did not know how much he should tell her.

'I understand you ... you were there. It was in the morning papers. What ... what happened?'

Briefly Eric told her of his visit to Castle Street, of what he had found, of how he had reacted. It was quickly told, and he related nothing of Arkwright's visit, or Gus Thomas's hypothesis.

'You went there after you left me, then?' she asked. He nodded, and she went on, 'So if you hadn't had ... an attack, you would have gone there that evening, and maybe she wouldn't have died.'

He stared at her. It was odd; she had put into words what had lain at the back of his mind, without expression, but now it was in the open. If he had gone there that evening and spoken to her, the killer might not have visited her. More, he might no longer have needed to kill her. Something of his thoughts appeared in his face, for Anne Morcomb said sharply, 'Are you all right?'

He stared at her, thinking back, coldly. There was no way in which he could feel guilty about what had happened, and yet he must bear a degree of responsibility. Woodenly he said, 'That's right. If I had gone there, she wouldn't have died... No, I'm all

195

right, Anne, I was just thinking of something else...'

'So you never got to speak to her in the end,' she said, after a little while.

He shook his head. 'Maybe she would have had no information anyway.'

'You don't think that, though, do you?' She was looking at him with real sympathy in her eyes. 'And now you feel you never will close to your satisfaction this Egan thing.'

Her sympathy broke through to him suddenly. He shook his head again. 'It's not just that. The fact is, I did know more than I told you out at Seddon Burn. And maybe Sarah Boden could have helped, maybe not. You see, Anne, I believe Arthur Egan never killed Colonel Denby. I believe he was merely protecting his half-brother – and he got railroaded by policemen who were eager for a conviction.'

Her eyes werc wide. 'I don't understand.'

He explained to her, telling her of Arkwright and Kenton, of Tiggy Williams and Jackie Parton's enquiries in Byker and Scotswood, and as he explained he saw the anger grow in her eyes, her mouth tighten with contempt for the manner in which the dead man had been treated. 'If this is true,' she almost exploded, 'you can't let things

196

rest there!'

'I don't see what else to do. There's no mileage in dragging it all up out of the past now; I'd gain some satisfaction in making Starling and the rest squirm, but that's all there would be to it. It could never be made public, because proof would be next to impossible, and I'd get sued for slander if I spoke out.'

'But it's so ... so *unfair!*' she cried.

'I agree. That men should do these things to Egan ... and that he should never really have defended himself, because he wanted to save his half-brother.'

'And *he* is beyond contempt, if what you say is true!' Her eyes were blazing now with suppressed anger. 'This man Andrews ... how he could possibly have allowed Egan to go to prison in his place is beyond my comprehension!'

'Well, it's what I *guess* happened, but I can't be sure, of course.'

'You're not going to let it end here, Eric, surely!'

He smiled at her vehemence. 'It'll never come out, you know – but no, I'm still going to make a few more enquiries. Now Sarah Boden is dead it's unlikely I'll find the beneficiaries to Egan's estate, so I'll wind it up now. But I've asked Jackie Parton to do a couple of things for me, and I still want to find out exactly what drew Egan to Vixen Hill.'

'Egan?' She was puzzled. 'I thought you said *Andrews* killed Colonel Denby.'

'That's right. But Egan went back to Vixen Hill himself several times, after he was released from prison.' He explained about Fred Bridges to her, and she shivered.

'It's an odd feeling. 'I've known Vixen Hill all my life, and spent happy times there with Michael and his aunt but to feel the place is central to all this about Arthur Egan ... it sort of changes things, the way you look at a place, doesn't it?'

He nodded. He still hadn't told her that it was likely Sarah Boden had been murdered, and he saw no reason to now. They sat silently for a little while, contemplatively, and then she stirred, as though about to go. Quickly he said, 'We're expecting counsel's opinion on the Inland Revenue case today.'

'Ah. Does that mean you'll be coming out to Sedleigh Hall again soon?'

'I expect so, unless your father wishes the meeting to be held here.'

She shook her head. 'No, that won't be possible. He's ... he's not well. I told you the other day. But it seems to me he's very down at the moment; quite weak, and not eating well. I'm ... I'm quite worried about him.' She frowned, looked up to him. 'David ... David Penrose and I had a long talk with him yesterday. It was about the Carlton Engineering thing, really. David and I, we're both of the same mind, and we thought we'd better see how he felt. I think we've half persuaded him that when he comes to raise the money to pay the death duties it would be best for everyone concerned to retain the land, keep this open-cast thing out of the area, and sell some of the portfolio his uncle left him when he died.'

Eric nodded. 'You're probably right. The only problem is his financial advisers might well suggest he'd be taking a pretty heavy loss on the shares. They're way down, and to unload such a large amount of stock at one time will depress the price even further.'

She shrugged unhappily. 'Six of one isn't it? Still, David's been very helpful.'

He thought he detected a certain defensiveness in her tone, and watched her carefully. 'I'm sure he's got your best interests at heart – and those of your father.'

'He's also a very patient man.'

'That's *usually* a recommendation,' Eric

said, and then, as a certain tightness developed in his chest, he added, 'I can think of some circumstances, however, where it would not be.'

She knew precisely what he meant, even though he only half understood what he was saying himself. Her eyes were still, her glance locked with his and a faint flush stained her cheek. They said nothing, and after a little while she rose, and he rose with her. In a small, puzzled voice, she said, 'I expect I'll see you when you come out to Sedleigh Hall.'

'I expect so.'

After she had gone he sat behind his desk and tried to bring some order to the thoughts that swirled around in his head. He was being foolish, that he knew. She was just an attractive young woman who had happened to cross his path; that's where it should end – that's where it must end. And yet she had made a considerable impact on him – and, it seemed, she was not impervious to his existence, either. But he could remember almost every moment of the brief times they had spent together so far, could remember almost every word she had said to him.

It was she who had suggested he talk to Sarah Boden, and if he did not tell her now of the suspicious nature of the old woman's death, that was merely to save her unhappiness and guilt. Because, after all, there was the possibility that Sarah Boden had died because ... because Eric Ward was coming to speak to her.

And it was Anne Morcomb who had sent Ward to the old woman. But no ... there was something else, another consideration he had not yet taken into account. When Anne Morcomb had given him Sarah's name, suggesting that he go and talk to her at Warkworth, there had been someone else present to hear the suggestion. One other person; the man who farmed Vixen Hill.

Eric Ward picked up a pencil and doodled the names, thoughtfully, on the blotting pad lying on his desk.

Vixen Hill ... Michael Denby.

2

Jackie Parton tried several times to make contact with Eric Ward the next day. Each time he received the same answer from the receptionist with the pert voice.

'I'm sorry, but Mr Ward is in conference at the moment and cannot be disturbed. Can I take a message?'

Stuff taking messages. They had a habit of getting lost.

The report he had to make was incomplete anyway: he just wanted to tell Eric what he'd picked up at Warkworth, and explain that he should soon be able to trace the owner of the black Ford with the crumpled wing.

The owner of the Northumberland Arms had been most co-operative, in the event.

It always helped if they were racing fans, and in this case the licensee had not only been a committed follower of the flats, he had also been an admirer of Jackie Parton ever since he'd picked up twenty quid for a shilling bet on Circe, Parton's fifth ride at Newcastle. So a couple of drinks and a bit of racing chat and there was no problem.

'Black Ford? Don't see many black cars around these days, do you? Black with a crumpled wing, you say? Why aye, that's it! Stays here from time to time, he does. Just the one night, usually. Chatted once or twice, we have. Says he likes the coast air and a walk down to the beach. Good walks along there, you know, Jackie, if you can take the wind in your face goin', wind up your backside comin'! Aye, he'll be the feller, 'cos he complained a few weeks back about that thump he'd caught in the wing. Happened here, when he was parked in the square, he reckoned. No time to fix it since, seems like.'

'You know his name?'

'He'll be registered, like. Want a look? Polis already had a look, and they been checking – not sure why, but rumour reckons it's to do with Sarah Boden's falling and dying, but why they'd want to check hotel registers I just don't know.'

Jackie had gone through the register, and the name was pointed out to him: *J. A. French*. Also included was the registered number of the car – not in the hotel register, but on a card French had filled in the last time he'd arrived and which had remained in the desk. Jackie had noted the number and then bought the landlord another beer at the lounge bar.

'What's he do here then, this feller French?' Jackie Parton asked.

'Businessman, seems like. Doesn't come up regular, he's from Newcastle way, he reckons, and only stays a day or so – morning walk sometimes, and in the evening he meets some feller or other.'

'He meets someone? Can you describe him?'

'Naw, can't say I could do that. I've seen them in the lounge – they don't come in the bar, but go in the residents' lounge. No one else ever uses that place since we moved the telly. So they two have a quiet chat there, I suppose, and get their drinks brought in.'

'And according to the register, he was in recently.'

'That's right. The same night Miss Boden died. The polis already asked about that.'

'Hmmm. And his friend ... did he turn up that night, too?'

The landlord had considered the matter for a while. 'Can't be sure. Think so. But I don't think they used the residents' lounge that night. His friend – the bloke he meets – he didn't stay long. We had some late bookings coming in, as I remember, and he left shortly after that.' When Jackie Parton pressed him, he came out with a time. 'Be about eight, maybe. We'd just started serving dinner. He'll have left then. Mr French, I think he just went to his room. Didn't take dinner, anyway.'

It was irritating not being able to contact Eric Ward. To start with, Jackie wanted to know if Ward knew the name J. A. French. And secondly, he wondered whether Eric Ward, who had stayed at the Northumberland Arms that night, had gone down to dinner.

At about eight in the evening.

The conference in which Eric Ward was involved proved to be exhausting. Joseph Francis had now decided to dispense with the services of his son Paul in the matter of *Morcomb v Inland Revenue Commissioners*. It did his temper no good, and it caused him to put more pressure on Eric Ward. In one sense Eric felt it to be unfair, for his position in the firm was still merely that of an articled clerk; at the same time, he realized that this was a golden opportunity for him to display his grasp of legal niceties in an important issue for the firm.

Joseph Francis had insisted that they went back, together, over the whole history of the estate duty litigation – and that meant rooting back to the period before Lord Morcomb had succeeded to his title, the estates and the shareholdings. The senior partner not only wanted his own memory refreshed; he wanted to be sure that when they were called upon to offer advice to Lord Morcomb it would be sound, practical, correct – and agreed advice.

'All right, Eric,' he said at last, 'let's summarize. I've digested counsel's opinion; you can take it away to bone up for Monday. Meanwhile, once again, the whole position.'

Eric went over it once again. He dealt with the abstracts of title, the commercial and mining transactions carried out on the estates, and referred in detail to the share certificates and transfers. Joseph Francis nodded. 'Fine. We may well be called upon to advise about possible sales of shares. There's one of them – Amalgamated Newfoundland Properties – they're way down, but I heard a rumour recently that they could jump sharply. And there's some holding company interested in them, too, for control purposes. Was it Western Consolidated? I don't know ... no matter... Go on.'

'That brings us to title. The deeds are ... here. The previous Lord Morcomb's will, with the two codicils annexed. His death in 1970 ... and the terms of his will, the entailed estate, the scheduled properties ... to go to the present Lord Morcomb and the heirs of his body.'

'Why they still use that phrase since the 1925 Act I don't know,' Francis grumbled. 'Only serves to confuse the layman. Anyway...'

'Included in the properties listed are those

held by the previous Lord Morcomb in his own right, and now included with all held by Lord Morcomb.'

'Very significant holdings too. Go on.'

'It all came to Lord Morcomb in 1970, and the first Inland Revenue claim is dated...' Eric paused. 'One thing, sir.'

'Yes?'

'The present Lord Morcomb was married twice. His second wife, Anne's mother, died, but—'

'Yes, yes, what's the problem?'

'I'm not sure whether his first marriage might have led to any claims to the estate. Certainly, I've found no record—'

'It's all right. There were no children of the first marriage.'

Eric Ward glanced helplessly through the files prior to 1971. 'But may not the first wife have some sort of claim that should be taken into account—'

Joseph Francis sighed impatiently. He smoothed back his hair, pinched with tired fingers at the bridge of his nose. 'Come on, Eric, you should have picked that up earlier. There was no issue of the first marriage. The second marriage is all we need concern ourselves with if we are going to bother at all about succession – though at this stage it's all a bit premature. But there was a settlement made in any case, on Lord Morcomb's first wife, after the nullity decree was obtained in 1950 or whenever it was. So you can forget her. The estate is now clear and unencumbered – and we can get down to the matter of counsel's opinion – if you really now do have the whole matter straight in your mind.'

Eric nodded. 'I think so. I'm pretty sure.'

With that, Joseph Francis was satisfied. He rose, yawning. 'All right. It's been a long day, so we'll leave it there. Now look, first thing on Monday you make your own way to Sedleigh Hall; be there by eleven for our conference with Lord Morcomb. Here's counsel's opinion for you to indulge in some weekend reading. I think you'll find ... well, read it for yourself and see what it says. And maybe consider just what kind of advice we ought to be giving Lord Morcomb on Monday.' He handed the slim folder to Eric and waved him to the door. 'So have a good weekend, and I'll see you Monday morning.'

As Eric reached the door, Joseph Francis called after him. 'By the way, you *have* got rid of the Egan administration, haven't you?'

'You said by Friday, sir.'

'And that,' Joseph Francis said positively,

'is today.'

The Egan administration.

The words meant very little to Eric any more. At the beginning it had meant a simple matter of succession to be resolved and dealt with in a matter of a couple of days work. But as time had passed and he had become more involved, drawn down a slippery slope he now had little idea of, the administration issue itself had become more and more relegated to the back of his mind as his concentration had moved towards the man Egan, his character, his lonely life, and the manner in which he had lived it. He felt anger, as did Anne Morcomb, and in his own way Jackie Parton too, for the injustices that had been heaped upon Arthur Egan. Dead or not, he deserved to have his truths be known.

And yet, though Eric was more than half convinced by the account he and Parton had derived together, and though he knew that Anne Morcomb had been impressed by the story he told her about Arthur Egan and Tommy Andrews and the older man protecting his half-brother for the actions and events at Vixen Hill, there was still something hollow at the heart of it all. There were times Eric thought he knew and understood Arthur Egan; but there were times too when he felt he knew nothing about him at all. There was still something at the core of the whole affair which eluded him: and it was something that concerned Vixen Hill. He was certain of it, for the farm seemed to be central to it all.

Yet there was no connection he could see, if it had indeed been Tommy Andrews who killed Colonel Denby at Vixen Hill.

He rolled over in bed, switched on the lamp and looked at his watch. Two o'clock in the morning. He turned off the light again and lay back but sleep was impossible. He was overtired perhaps, as a result of the long session with Joseph Francis on the Morcomb case, but there was also the feeling that he was still missing something of importance in the Egan affair. He should not be bothering about it; he should now finish it, it was all long dead and gone, and the connection between Sarah Boden and Arthur Egan was fanciful. But he could not let it rest.

Jackie Parton was checking on the man in the black Ford. What if that man turned out to be Tommy Andrews? They could not *know* the man was dead. Eric had seen him in the neighbourhood of Vixen Hill and

Sedleigh Hall, and his car had been present at Warkworth on the night Sarah Boden had died. If it had been Andrews, what still drew him back to the Denby farm? And what had he been doing in Warkworth, on the night the old woman had been murdered?

Murdered.

Eric rose, padded downstairs in bare feet and made himself a hot drink before going into his study and picking up the Egan file yet again. He was vaguely alarmed by his obsession and yet could find no rest from the questions that plagued him. He opened the file and took out the contents: the envelope with the blond hair; the letter from Fred Bridges; the photographs.

The photographs. He stared at them until the images began to dance before his eyes. The young Arthur Egan; the younger Tommy Andrews. The baby. And the gravestone; the churchyard.

It was the one avenue he had not explored. He had tried everything else. Perhaps the answer lay there.

He finished his drink and then went back to bed. But it was almost dawn before he drifted back to sleep. And when he did, he dreamed, and his dreams were full of dark cypress trees, and the stark, gaunt shape of a Norman tower.

The telephone woke him at eight o'clock. He had no bedside extension so had to stumble, bleary-eyed, down the stairs to the hallway. Before he reached the phone it went dead and he cursed. Now he was up, tired or not, there was no point in going back to bed. He would not be able to sleep. He made himself a light breakfast and sat down to read the newspaper.

At nine-thirty the telephone rang again. It was Jackie Parton, grumbling at the difficulty he was having in contacting Ward.

'What is it you want, Jackie?' Ward asked shortly.

'Nothin' *I* want. Just reporting, that's all. Traced that black Ford chap you was on about. Name's French. Ring a bell?'

'None.'

'Maybe it's not his real name, of course. Or he could have changed it some time,' Parton said carefully.

There was a short silence, as though each waited for the other to speak, to say what lay in both their minds. It was Parton who finally said it. 'This feller ... he was in Warkworth that night. He *could* be Tommy Andrews, Eric.'

Eric Ward's lips were dry. 'I think that's

taking our suppositions too far – and it doesn't make sense, anyway.'

'All I'm saying is, it could be,' Parton insisted. 'So we ought to go a bit canny, you know? I got a pal checking the car registration, but he's having some difficulty. Weekends is awkward, He did get a quick look at the file, and he thinks it's a *company* registration, but he's going to let me know by Monday. Now where can I contact you?'

'First thing Monday I'll be driving to Sedleigh Hall. If it's urgent, try me there – but I'll be back late afternoon I expect.'

'Living high these days, Eric, hey? All right that'll be okay – but ... er ... stay tight, you know what I mean?'

'I know what you mean.'

Parton rang off and Eric tried to finish the newspaper but his mind kept drifting off at a tangent. Tommy Andrews. He could hardly believe the man he had seen was Egan's younger half-brother – but it was possible. They would be of the same age ... but what would he be doing at Warkworth, and near Vixen Hill?

He kept coming back to the same problem. But if there *was* a link between the past and the present Tommy Andrews might be that link. And if he was, Eric remembered,

213

the man might well have killed once – now perhaps, twice.

At Vixen Hill and Warkworth.

Vixen Hill.

He was sure the key lay there, and yet last night he had wondered whether it might be in the churchyard photograph. He wandered through to his study and looked at the photographs again, then, deciding suddenly he went back to the phone and dialled the Newcastle City Library. They prided themselves on answering any reasonable question. His was relatively simple.

'I want to get in touch with anyone who is regarded as an authority on local churches – in Northumberland that is.'

To range more widely would be foolish. This enquiry, at least, was going to be finite, and if there was no answer forthcoming that would be the end of it all.

The library rang back an hour later. They could suggest a name – someone who actually worked in the library itself, and he would be quite happy to see Mr Ward on this Saturday provided he presented himself before four o'clock.

Ward called at John Dobson Street at precisely half past two.

The librarian was tall, fair, immensely

enthusiastic about his specialism and non-plussed for perhaps half an hour. While he sorted through a box of files he kept in his small, claustrophobic workroom he kept up a flow of chatter, directed towards informing Eric that in his opinion Northumberland had perhaps the finest heritage of churches in the country. There were those who might extol the virtues of other counties, the Midlands, the South West, but in his view Northumberland was prime, with its peel towers, its Norman arches, its castle chapels. 'Ovingham,' he said, interrupting himself. 'Or ... maybe Hartburn.' He was holding a small collection of sketches in his hand. 'Eighteenth-century, these sketches – the originals, that is. These are copies, of course. But that tower in the photograph Ovingham, Hartburn ... or, just possibly, Ogle. I think, Mr Ward, that's as near as I could get. And I would have loved to come out with you to look – any excuse, you see, to visit such delightful buildings, but this weekend I'm booked to visit, yet again, the cathedral at York. Makes a change, you know? And they're doing such interesting work there...'

Ward thanked him, and left.

Ovingham, Hartburn, or Ogle.

They were all within striking distance of

215

Newcastle and armed with the photograph he drove straight out on to the Jedburgh Road.

Two hours later he found the church he was seeking, at Hartburn.

The setting was delightful. A cluster of cottages adorned the hill, some tastefully modernized, near the tiny square and the neat sward leading down to the church. The road dipped sharply past the church and swung into a bend that rose steeply once it crossed the stream that meandered through the meadows below the church walls. Ward walked past the vicarage, strangely reluctant to enter the churchyard itself, not knowing what he might find there, and in some odd way afraid both of success and disappointment. Either way, he feared a sense of anticlimax and he was emotionally unprepared for it. It had only been a matter of weeks, but his obsession with Arthur Egan had become so intense that now its possible end stretched his nerves in an inexplicable manner.

Then, telling himself he was foolish, he turned back and walked through the lychgate into the churchyard.

He walked along the narrow path and realized that some of the tombstones were very old: lichen sent grey roses over the lettering, making it almost indecipherable and on some of the older stones the action of rain and frost had split the surfaces until long sections of stone had simply peeled away. Eighteenth-century naval captains lay beside child victims of the cholera and on one group of stones a skull and crossbones appeared, a Masonic trademark, Ward assumed.

He looked again at the blurred photographs and sought the cypress trees. They lay in the west corner of the churchyard so he walked towards them and then, turning his back to them, made his way down the sloping ground to the far corner of the churchyard. In the corner a hedge of wild rose barred the way to the steep scarp slope down to the stream below, and in this corner, where the late afternoon sun shone, the graves were more recent than those which appeared at the front of the church. He looked at the photograph again, then turned. The sun was in his eyes and he raised a hand, shading against the glare.

It would have to be near here, according to the photograph that Arthur Egan had kept in his wallet as a remembrance. The grave of a child, perhaps, or of his half-brother... Soon, Eric Ward would know, and there was a constriction in his chest as he walked slowly among the tombstones, reading the inscriptions, searching for one that would have significance for him.

Yet when it came, for perhaps three seconds it had no significance. He stopped, stared at it, and puzzlement distorted logical thought. He checked with the photograph, stepped back, crouched down as the photographer must have done to take the picture, and then he rose and walked close to the stone again. There could be no doubt; it was the stone that appeared in the photograph.

Eric Ward stood there for almost twenty minutes thereafter, thinking. Gradually, logic reasserted itself, and he pieced it all together, the loneliness, the hurt, the painful longing felt by the quiet, reserved man in Westerhope. The years in prison and the years thereafter, they would all have been the same for him, and when he had been released he had come here, to take this photograph. It was all he had left to him – that, and a lock of blond hair.

And Vixen Hill. Eric Ward could understand Vixen Hill now, and perhaps the twenty thousand pounds too. It all fitted, all pieced together, as soon as he saw the tombstone.

He remembered what ex-Detective Inspector Kenton had said: all they needed against Egan, to put him away, was the clinching evidence, and it was Arkwright who had supplied it, under Superintendent Starling's direction.

Eric Ward had had the pieces of this puzzle in front of him for days. He hadn't been able to recognize them for what they were, or fit them together, until this one clinching piece of evidence had reached him. The one thing that made sense out of it all, that tied it all together.

He did not know the truth about Arthur Egan, but he could guess. And he knew now how to find the truth, and where it lay.

Chapter Six

1

They sat in the library, around a polished mahogany table and coffee was served. The maid moved softly, discreetly, dispensing the coffee from a silver service, and the late morning sun slanted through the mullioned windows, sending a bar of light across the table, picking out the gold lettering on the spines of the books scattered in front of Joseph Francis and the man on his left. Eric Ward sat opposite them, to one side of David Penrose, and once again he was struck by the contrasts that his professional life involved him in: the quiet, expensive elegance of Sedleigh Hall, and the narrow, cramped terraces of the Scotswood Road.

'You seem preoccupied this morning, Mr Ward,' David Penrose said quietly.

Ward managed a smile. 'I was really just enjoying being here. It's a world away from Newcastle.'

'You don't need to tell me that,' Penrose replied. 'Don't be fooled by my accent – I had to work at it. When I was a child this wasn't my kind of scene at all. But I've been lucky, and I'm here – and it certainly is my intention never to go back.' He glanced at Ward suddenly, as though aware that he might have communicated something he should not have done. 'This is the summit of my ambition, you see – to live and work at Sedleigh Hall.'

Ward thought about Anne Morcomb and wasn't so sure. He sipped his coffee, and said, 'That's nice, anyway, to reach the summit of your ambition at your age.'

'Aren't you achieving yours?' Penrose asked.

Ward shrugged. 'I don't know that I have much ambition any more. A secure future in the law: that'll do.' His eyes strayed to Joseph Francis, carrying on a desultory conversation with the man sitting near him. A secure future ... even that could not be certain.

The clock chimed eleven, and the doors to the library opened as though they had been awaiting this moment. Lord Morcomb stood in the entrance, leaning on his daughter's arm. 'You will forgive me, gentlemen, but I am advised I should not join you this morning.'

He was ill. The skin of his face, which had seemed leathery to Ward, now possessed a translucent pallor; the colour seemed to have faded from his pouched eyes and with the colour had gone the hard coldness that had so impressed earlier. The line of his jaw seemed to have slackened, folds of skin hanging loosely at his neck, and the hand on his daughter's arm was ridged with veins that ran stiff under tightly stretched skin.

They rose; Joseph Francis setting the example, the others following. 'My lord, if you think this conference should be postponed–'

'No.' Lord Morcomb's voice was soft and

husky, but positive enough. 'This thing's been going on too long. I want decisions today ... get it resolved. Anne my daughter will join you in a few minutes. It's as much her concern as mine, so her presence will suffice and she can report to me later. Now, if you'll excuse me...'

Anne Morcomb was looking at Eric Ward. Her glance was shadowed – she had caught something in his eyes, something he had not wanted to express. Then she was turning away with her father, and the doors closed behind them. Eric sat down. 'He looks very ill,' he said.

'Yes.' Penrose was staring at Ward speculatively. 'I think he's dying. He's not been well for some days ... and he's getting weaker. I think this whole Inland Revenue thing has got him down. Certainly, since the last time you were here, he's hardly left his room. Getting weaker steadily. And this is the first time he's ever missed a meeting as important as this.' He paused, pushed aside his coffee cup. 'Have you met Anne yet?'

Ward was not deceived by the casual tone of Penrose's voice. 'A few times. Michael Denby introduced us, in the first instance, at Vixen Hill.'

'Ah yes,' Penrose replied absently. 'I do

recall her telling me, now. She ... she's very worried about her father.' He looked at Ward almost challengingly, but the question remained unspoken, and then Joseph Francis broke in to suggest that they might set aside the coffee cups and prepare for Anne Morcomb's return.

She came in some minutes later. She moved, a little self-consciously, towards the seat her father would have taken at the head of the table and then, gaining in confidence, asked if they had all met each other. She formally introduced the bespectacled man on Joseph Francis's left as Mr Henried, her father's financial adviser and member of a stock-broking firm in Newcastle. 'Now, the purpose of the conference today is, essentially, to discuss the estate duty issues. I assume we'll be here for some hours, so I've arranged for lunch to be available. Do you wish to start, Mr Francis?'

He was happy to do so. He began, for the benefit of Mr Henried, by covering ground familiar to several of them: the position of the Morcomb estates prior to 1970, the land and shareholdings of the previous Lord Morcomb were detailed, and schedules were produced to distinguish between those properties which came to the present Lord

223

Morcomb as of right, and those which fell in to him as a result of the will of his uncle. With some questions from Mr Henried, and some interventions from Eric Ward, the morning wore away. At one-thirty Anne Morcomb suggested they adjourn for sherry, and lunch.

Having abjured the sherry, Eric felt he could accept a glass of white wine that was served with the cold collation; afterwards, as they all stood on the terrace in the sunshine, taking some fresh air before they returned to the library, Eric walked down into the sunken garden, among the rose-bushes, alone. His head was aching, and he feared he might have another attack today. It was not due merely to the work he had done on the Morcomb file: he still had questions to ask, decisions to make. It all amounted to tension, and pressure.

Anne Morcomb was standing on the terrace when he returned. She was alone. She stood watching him as he walked towards her and when he reached the terrace, she said 'The others have gone into the library. 'Are ... are you all right, Eric?'

He smiled. 'Of course. Why do you ask?'

She wasn't fooled. 'You seemed preoccupied this morning. And ... tired. You've been working hard at our business?'

'Hard enough.'

'And the Arthur Egan thing?'

He looked away from her, at the terrace, at the lawns and meadows beyond, at the quarry scarring the hillside, and he nodded. 'It's all but finished now.' He turned back to her dismissively. 'Your father isn't well.'

Anxiety shadowed her eyes. She nodded. 'The doctor's seen him several times. There's nothing specifically wrong, he says – rest should cure him. But I get the feeling it's as though he doesn't really want to recover. Like a machine wearing out, you know? The parts don't function any more, not properly, and Daddy, seems almost ... reconciled to just drifting away. I don't understand it, Eric.'

He hesitated. 'Would it be possible for me to see him?' She was startled. She stared at him for several seconds.

'Is it important?'

'I think so.'

'I don't really know whether ... I'll speak to him. The doctor will be calling again at four – I'll have a word with him, too. What ... why do you want to see him?'

He pursed his lips and avoided her glance. There was a short silence. Coolly she said at last, 'We'd better go into the library to join the others.'

When he took his seat he was conscious of the fact that David Penrose was very aware that Anne had waited for him on the terrace.

Joseph Francis began the afternoon session by calling upon Eric Ward. 'We have now received counsel's opinion, and perhaps Eric could put it into suitable language and perspective.'

Eric nodded. 'Counsel refers to the authorities of *Ellesmere v Inland Revenue Commissioners; the Marr's Trustees Case;* and the *Duke of Buccleuch v Inland Revenue Commissioners,* but I won't go through the detailed exposition of principle that he deals with in those cases. Instead, I'll attempt a brief summary of what he says, and let you have a few of his quotations.'

'That's right,' David Penrose murmured. 'Remember we're no lawyers.'

'The basic facts in issue between Lord Morcomb and the Inland Revenue concern the method of assessment for the purposes of calculation of estate duty. Counsel points out that the words of section 7(5) of the Finance Act 1894 are quite clear and explicit. I quote:

The principal value of any property shall be estimated to be the price which, in the opinion of the Commissioners, such property would fetch if sold in the open market at the time of the death of the deceased.

It is the contention of the Commissioners that they have done precisely that. Lord Morcomb, in turn, raises two counter arguments. He suggests, firstly, that the sum should be reduced to take account of the impossibility of offering for sale at the time of death all the property as individual estates.'

Joseph Francis turned to Mr Henried. 'It's an argument about reasonableness – if the sale were negotiated, it would have to be at a reduced price, to allow for speculation and profit taking and so on.'

'Yes, I see, I see,' Henried replied, making notes as Eric went on.

'The second argument Lord Morcomb has raised concerned the sale at time of death – that is, the death of the previous Lord Morcomb in 1970. He contends this ought to be construed as a reasonable period after the time of death – once again, because such a hypothetical sale would be a practical impossibility for the simple reason sales of such magnitude could not be achieved – at least, not without some considerable loss to the estate.'

'I understand that,' Henried said.

Eric turned to look at Anne Morcomb; she was watching him, and there was a shadow of anxiety still in her glance. 'I won't give you the detailed analysis counsel has raised in his opinion, nor will I use the references he makes to specific points in the Act and in the decided cases. I'll simply summarize what, in effect, he says. And essentially, it's quite simple. If the Inland Revenue Commissioners were to take the steps advocated by Lord Morcomb, they would be acting in disobedience of the clear directions of section 7(5) of the 1894 Act. Words of an Act of Parliament cannot be paraphrased so as to take on what would be, essentially, a new meaning. Accordingly, counsel is of the opinion that the hypothetical sale of the Hardford Estate is quite consistent with the criteria for valuation laid down in section 7.' He paused, glanced around the table to make sure they were all following the argument. 'In other words, Lord Morcomb's arguments are unlikely to be supported in the House of Lords; the Commissioners have acted correctly; the basis for valuation of the Hardford Estate is correct – and the liability for death duties is properly based on the figure of three million plus, and not the lower figure proposed by Lord Morcomb.' He sat back, folded his arms, and waited.

There was a short silence, then David Penrose let out his breath in a long sigh. 'So this is the end of the line, on the appeals.'

'That is the recommendation of counsel,' Eric agreed.

'And would you go along with the recommendation?' Anne Morcomb asked sharply.

Eric glanced at Joseph Francis; with a sight inclination of his head the senior partner directed him to answer. 'Let's put it like this. No one's infallible. The Inland Revenue Commissioners employ sound lawyers. We've now asked the opinion of a leading barrister – and he gives you the same story as the Commissioners are saying. That doesn't prevent you going to the House of Lords on appeal. But it's going to cost money – and it's likely to fail. My ... our advice would be, accept this opinion. Give up the fight.'

'My father...'

Her words died away as David Penrose caught her glance. 'We ought to be realistic,' he said quietly, and she nodded, after a brief hesitation, capitulating.

They sat there for a little while silently,

waiting for Anne Morcomb to speak. At last, quietly, she said, 'My father has given me full authority to make decisions this afternoon which he will regard as binding. There will, of course, be opportunity later for proper documents to be signed by Lord Morcomb, but for the time being we need to decide what action must be taken. You will all be aware that it is not so much the different valuation that was of importance – though it was significant enough. There was also the question of delay. It will not be easy, in the short term, to raise sufficient money to pay the death duties falling on the estate. We now need to decide, therefore, how the money is to be raised, since the moment we step back from our decision to pursue the issues to the House of Lords we effectively concede the point to the Inland Revenue Commissioners and thus become liable for the payments.'

Henried cleared his throat. 'I think I should come in here. I won't go into details, though the facts are in these portfolios here. The situation, simply, is this. To meet the liabilities for death duties you must either sell a considerable part of your land holdings, or else you must relinquish a large part of your shareholdings.'

'And what would your advice be in that

respect, Mr Henried?'

'The portfolio developed by the late Lord Morcomb was a peculiar one. It contained very few company holdings, in fact – and these were somewhat speculative, to say the least. The present state of the market shows these holdings to be at a low ebb; a significant sale of the shares would also produce a fall in prices. I would not be happy, therefore, to sell in a falling market. I would press consideration of the other alternative.'

'The sale of land,' David Penrose said. 'I don't think that's on.'

Henried fluttered his hands in concern. 'I fail to see–'

'The basic problem outlined in Lord Morcomb's arguments with the Commissioners applies,' Penrose said sharply. 'We couldn't find a buyer to pick up large slices of our land here – not otherwise than at giveaway prices. The estate would lose a considerable portion of its holdings – and in my view, land is something you need to hold on to. It's always there – not like shareholdings which can rise in value, or fall, overnight.' Eric Ward was surprised at the vehemence in his tone, but Penrose hadn't finished. 'Apart from that, there's only one buyer at the moment who would be interested in picking up large sections of Morcomb land. And even if we had time – which we don't – that buyer might still come in heavy and get what is desired.'

'Mr Penrose is referring to a company called Carlton Engineering,' Anne Morcomb explained. 'I have discussed the matter with him at considerable length and I agree with his views. We have certain responsibilities in this area of the county, responsibilities which would not be discharged if we allowed a company like this one to come in and scar the landscape, change the life of the inhabitants–'

'I can't quite agree,' Henried murmured. 'They would also produce work – that is, if they ever did what they say they want to do. I have some doubts indeed whether they are truly interested at all in the Morcomb estates. My contacts in the City suggest–'

'I wonder what our legal brothers feel about it?' Penrose interrupted harshly.

Once again, Joseph Francis gave Eric his baptism of fire. He raised an eyebrow, leaving the field to Eric, who cleared his throat nervously. 'I've looked at the holdings. There are complications. Some of the land-holdings could not be sold without some difficulty. The proceeds could not be used to clear death duties because the estates are entailed, to Lord Morcomb and the heirs of his body.

The rest would be the land in which Carlton Engineering would seem to be interested. On balance, therefore, it seems to me dispersal of some of the shareholdings would be best.'

'And in particular,' Penrose said quickly, 'the holdings in Amalgamated Newfoundland Properties. They're never going to be at a better price, and they would in no way unbalance what is a pretty unbalanced portfolio anyway.'

Eric Ward stared at him in some surprise. David Penrose seemed particularly well versed in the holdings of the Morcomb estate, for a mere estate manager. Then he caught Anne Morcomb's glance fixed on David Penrose, and realized that Penrose was more than just an estate manager. He had the confidence, and perhaps more, of Anne Morcomb.

The afternoon wore on as Henried expounded on the detailed holdings of the estate. Strictly speaking, it was not within the brief held by Francis, Shaw and Elder, but since they would be called upon to carry out the legal procedures consequent upon the decisions taken, the senior partner and the articled clerk stayed on. When tea was served, however, Joseph Francis drew Eric to one side, congratulated him briefly on his summary of counsel's opinion and then suggested that while he might conveniently withdraw at this stage, it would be useful if Eric could stay on to the end of the meeting.

Eric agreed, Joseph made his apologies and left, and the meeting went on, after a short period when Anne left the room, presumably to see the doctor who had been expected at four. At six o'clock the decisions were finally taken. Henried would, as soon as possible, put the shareholding of Amalgamated Newfoundland Properties on the market, and Francis, Shaw and Elder would undertake the necessary legal procedures to sell the shares, transfer the certificates, and then negotiate with the Inland Revenue for the payment of death duties, after complete valuation on the basis of the principles applied already. Henried said goodbye and left; David Penrose stood up, stretched and walked over to Anne.

'I'm sure we've done the right thing,' he said, and that he was convinced was obvious from the note of exultation in his voice. 'But my head's splitting now – I need some fresh air. I'll see you this evening?'

She nodded. 'You're expected at dinner. Michael's coming over too.'

David Penrose pressed her hand and over

his shoulder her glance met Eric Ward's. Penrose nodded toward him and then left the library, walking quickly. Anne Morcomb moved towards Eric as he stood gathering up his papers.

'So that's all settled, then.'

He nodded. 'I think it's probably the right decision – provided you had all the facts at your disposal.'

'What do you mean?'

Ward shrugged. 'I don't know. Henried wasn't too happy. And he seemed to have some doubts about the Carlton intentions.'

She smiled. 'Mr Henried is concerned only with money; I have other responsibilities. I talked to you about them. This, I think, is the best way to discharge them... However, I've seen the doctor, Eric.'

'Yes?'

'He doesn't think it would be a good idea if Daddy saw anyone tonight. Mornings are his best time. He's sleeping now... You haven't told me why you want to see him.'

'No.'

'It's about Arthur Egan, and Vixen Hill, isn't it?'

He looked at her, wanting to say no more but knowing that he had to do so. He knew he could walk away right now, not see the old man upstairs, and perhaps it was the wisest thing to do, but he had started this thing, it had become an obsession with him, and now he wanted to know the truth. He was almost there; he wanted merely confirmation of the fact that Arthur Egan had been sent to prison for a crime he did not commit and then, perhaps, it would be over. Slowly he nodded. 'A few questions, that's all. And then...'

'In the morning, then,' she said softly. 'After all, it was I who told you to finish the thing, wasn't it?'

'I'll call around eleven—'

'No.' She hesitated, half turned away from him so that he could not see her eyes. 'It's been a long day and I've been watching you. You're tired. It would be far more sensible – rather than have you drive away and back again in the morning – if you stayed here tonight. It would be no problem.'

'I can hardly do that. I—'

'Michael Denby is coming to dinner this evening. He could, in other circumstances, have chosen a better time, but he'd heard Daddy was ill. He and David will be there, with me. I'd be happy if you could join us.'

She looked at him again, then, and he knew there was more to this than mere kindness on her part. There was something she wanted to know, and this would be her way of finding out.

2

Dinner turned out to be a more stilted affair than Eric had expected. Anne Morcomb seemed preoccupied and though David Penrose introduced an air of gaiety, seemingly at the top of his form, she made little response, and Michael Denby, whose eyes had expressed surprise at Eric's presence, also seemed rather morose. Dinner was also interrupted by a phone call from Jackie Parton, which Eric took in the library.

'Eric? Really slumming these days, aren't you!'

'It's the middle of dinner, Jackie.'

'Sorry, I'm sure. All right, I'll be quick. First of all, Tommy Andrews. I think we're really going to draw a blank there.'

'How do you mean?'

'I've now had information that he was killed in a brawl in Buenos Aires, maybe ten years ago. Can't be certain, of course, but this feller is prepared to swear... So it looks like there'll be no heirs of Arthur Egan to track down. One thing is certain – this French feller – he's not Tommy Andrews, as I had a kind of suspicion he might be.'

'Who is he, then?'

'He works for Carlton Engineering.'

'Carlton Engineering?' Eric was puzzled. 'What was he doing at Warkworth, then, and Vixen Hill?'

'Can't answer, old son. But ... get back to your dinner, hey? All I can say is, that black Ford is registered with the firm I mentioned.'

When he put the phone down Eric stood in the library for a few minutes, puzzled. Carlton Engineering. Where did they fit into all this? Michael Denby was concerned that the company might be interested in Vixen Hill, slicing his farm in two. But there was something else as well ... a rumour that Joseph Francis had heard.

Somehow, it disturbed him; it had some reference to decisions that had been taken today. Something, somewhere didn't quite fit.

His head was beginning to ache. He returned to the dining-room and listened to the desultory conversation, tried to take part in it but all the while the half-understood questions whirled around inside his head. He was missing a key – and at a time when he had other, more important issues on his mind, such as the projected interview with Lord Morcomb. Suddenly, he felt he wanted an end to it all; he wished he had agreed not to stay. He wished he had not gone out to Hartburn; he wished he had not decided to confront Lord Morcomb with old, buried, half-forgotten lies.

He realized Michael Denby was speaking to him. 'I'm sorry?'

'I asked you how things were going with your Egan administration thing.' Michael Denby's moroseness might have been a reflection of his feelings at the illness of his landlord, Lord Morcomb; it might have been the result of something else. Right now, however, he seemed to have taken a little too much wine, for his glance was blurred, his tone a little unsteady, hovering on the belligerent. 'You won't know about Egan, David. He murdered my father, you see, and now he's dead and Eric is still trying to find out things about him, but exactly what I'm no longer certain. But how is it going, Eric, how is it going?'

Eric Ward averted his eyes. 'It's about finished,' he said aware of the constricting band that seemed to be encircling his forehead.

'Closing the file? Well, what's happened? What have you found out?'

'I don't think—'

'Lawyers are always so close-mouthed,' Denby sneered. 'This is discreet company.' He grimaced towards Anne. 'We can be trusted to keep quiet, can't we?'

David Penrose leaned forward, his dark eyes concerned. In a soothing tone, he said, 'Mike, I really don't think this is the time—'

Michael Denby glared at him. 'What the hell do you know about it? Egan murdered my father. For years I've wondered about the man who killed him, what kind of bastard he was, and now I think I have every right to know just what Eric has been uncovering about him!'

'One of the things he's uncovered,' Anne said quickly, to Eric's dismay, 'is that Egan probably didn't kill your father after all!'

There was a silence, and Michael Denby's flushed face turned first to Anne, then to Eric Ward. He found some difficulty getting the words out. 'Egan? But of course he killed the Colonel. Damn it, he did seven years for it!'

'We think—' Eric caught the swift glance that David Penrose shot towards her as she used the word 'we' – 'that it wasn't Egan at all. He had a half-brother of whom he was fond. It was that man who killed your father, and Egan covered up for him.'

'To the extent of going to prison? That's a bit far-fetched!'

'He had other reasons too,' Eric said.

'Such as?' Denby challenged.

Eric made no reply. He wanted an end to this conversation. His head was aching still, and he felt shivery, slightly nauseous. 'No matter,' he said shortly. 'Let's leave it that he was prepared to serve a term of imprisonment rather than shop his younger half-brother. It doesn't matter anyway—'

'Doesn't matter?' Denby looked around the table in mock helplessness. 'I never went a bundle on my father, but I always had more than a little bit of hate in me for Arthur Egan! Now you say I should have been concentrating on someone else, and it doesn't matter? You're no great psychologist, Eric, believe me! What you've said only whets my appetite. What the hell have you found out?'

Anne was looking at him, half expectantly, half sympathetically. To help him, she turned to Michael Denby placatingly. 'The fact is, it seems he was prepared to do this to save his half-brother, and it suited the police also – they planted certain evidence that helped convict him—'

'Anne, you can't believe that,' Denby protested, 'It's getting even more ludicrous than ever! You mean there was a conspiracy to put Egan inside, and he went along with it? I've not heard anything so ridiculous in my life, and if–'

'That's precisely what happened,' Eric Ward snapped. The sickness was rising in his stomach, and his eyes were beginning to burn, 'And that's one of the reasons why I want to see Lord Morcomb!'

Anne's head turned; she was staring at him. David Penrose leaned forward. 'What's Lord Morcomb got to do with it?'

The cat was beginning to sharpen her claws; the first stabs of almost delicious agony were beginning to touch the back of his eyeballs. He heard Michael Denby say something, but he could not make out the words. He rose sharply, apologizing when his chair went over backwards and then he was hurrying from the room as the unsheathed claws ripped at him in that old, familiar, horrifying way. He stumbled up to his room, closed the door behind him, took out the fluid and applied it, his hands shaking, then lay back on his bed, waiting for the sickness and the nausea and the pain to pass.

It did not; it receded, but he felt the claws were still there, waiting, and then he must have fallen asleep for when the light knocking woke him he glanced at his watch, and saw that some two hours had passed. He rose, went to the door, and opened it.

It was Anne Morcomb.

'Are you all right?'

He nodded. 'I'm sorry. I upset your dinner-party.'

'It was hardly a cheerful one to begin with. It ... it was an attack?'

'Yes. A bad one. I'm sorry.'

'No. You've no reason to apologize.' She moved closer, her face in shadow for he had not turned on his bedroom light. 'What ... what was it you meant about Daddy?'

'I didn't mean–' He shook his head. Words were difficult to come by; they were dangerous. He was still thick-headed, not controlling his speech.

'Is that why you wanted to see him in the morning? Does he have some connection with Egan, and Vixen Hill? What's it all about, Eric?'

He shook his head stubbornly. He had to see Lord Morcomb first, to clear his suspicions. He felt her take his hands. 'Was Daddy behind Egan's being sent to prison? I must know–'

'I don't know that, Anne,' he said, wanting desperately to relieve her distress. 'I'm confused myself, particularly now. I don't know the real connections between Egan and your father, any more than I know why Sarah Boden was killed, but I have suspicions, guesses about some of it that only your father can explain.'

Her hands fell away from his. There was a short silence.

Then he heard the horror in her voice. 'You said Sarah was killed.'

He almost groaned aloud. He was in no condition to be cross-questioned. 'Please,' he said. 'In the morning, after I've seen your father. Then we can talk.'

After a while she touched his hands again. 'All right,' she said softly. 'Michael is just going; David will go soon. You get some sleep now, and we'll talk again. In the morning.'

He heard the door close quietly behind her, and he was in darkness again.

It brought him no relief. First of all, he felt the waves or nausea begin to come back to him, intermittently; then there was the dull throb of pain, difficult to locate, temples, eyes, but persistent. Normally, the pilocarpine did its work within fifteen minutes and then there was only the shuddering. Tonight, it was different. He had had one attack like this previously: the thought of another agonized him. He walked to the window and looked out. A full moon rode the night sky, above scudding clouds, but the tell-tale halo surrounded it, a diffusion caused by the gathering fluids in his eyes. He went back to the bed and lay down again, still fully dressed, waiting, but it was still there, almost predatory.

In another room in this great house an old man lay, ill like himself, perhaps dying. He knew the secrets which Ward almost knew ... and yet more too, the intertwining of so many secrets, a murder, a vanished half-brother, a lost child, a long, long silence after what had happened at Vixen Hill. A quiet grave in a village miles away from here.

The room was oppressive. He tried to make out the time by his watch but his eyesight was blurred and he dared not put on the light. He rose, and walked unsteadily to the door, sickness rising to his throat, and he wanted to be outside, in the night air, where he might get relief. He walked down the stairs, saw the misty light creeping under the library door and walked past. He thought he heard someone moving in the library but stumbled on, opening the main doors and walking out into the night air.

It was fresh and cool to his skin, touching his burning eyelids with soft fingers, and he moved carefully down the steps, down to the gravel of the parking area, across the soft, damp grass beyond. He felt the breeze in his face, caressing him, and he turned into it, aware of brightness of the moon and the deep shadows of the trees about him, but careless of the route he took, conscious only of the pain that lay behind his eyes. He walked for a few minutes and found himself in a lane; he stopped, leaning against a barred gate and looked about him, half dazed. He could make out haloed lights on the hill – Sedleigh Hall. He would walk on a little way more, in the cool evening; then he would retrace his steps, try another dose of pilocarpine before lying down to rest. He did not want to use the damned stuff too much – he felt it would be dangerous, but when the pain came again, in earnest...

He walked on again slowly, and the trees shadowed his progress under the moon.

To his left he was aware of fields, stretching out silently, further than he could see. Ahead of him the hill rose, fading against the stars. It was time to turn back.

But he was not alone.

He had known it for some time, without

recognizing or accepting the fact, his senses blurred and unresponsive by the drugged pain. Now, as he decided to turn back the awareness came to him sharply, and he swung around, peering back the way he had come. There was nothing he could make out, just trees and the narrow lane, but the cat stretched lazily again behind his eyes and he shuddered. He started to retrace his steps, his footsteps scraping the gravelly lane, and then he caught a brief glimpse of something dark moving away from the trees to his left and he stopped.

The shotgun barrel tapped lightly on his shoulder, just below his left ear. 'You make things easy, my friend,' the voice whispered and Eric Ward, through a haze of climbing pain, knew this would be how Fred Bridges would have come upon Arthur Egan in the darkness.

The shotgun nudged his left ear. 'Turn again, Whittington.' The pressure increased, making him turn around to face the hill again and then it slipped back, to press lightly against the nape of his neck. 'All right, you were walking. So walk.'

Ward stumbled forward, bemused by surprise and pain and the effects of the drug. He moved awkwardly, the shotgun jolting against the back of his neck, and he had walked several paces before he managed to speak. 'What the hell is this? I'm no poacher.'

'A matter of opinion,' the man behind him said, still half whispering. 'But I'll settle for investigator. You should have got the police out of your system, my friend. You should have stuck with the law?'

'Where are we going?'

'Just walk.'

They walked. Ward's head was throbbing now and the nausea that had gripped him earlier was rising again. He managed to continue for perhaps another fifty yards and then he suddenly stopped, leaning sideways as he retched violently. He heard the man behind him mutter in disgust, 'God, you are a mess.'

But the shotgun barrel prodded him again, a moment later, and they were climbing the hill, under the trees. 'What's this all about?' Ward asked again, his voice sounding hollow in his own skull. 'Why are you taking me up here?'

'Because I heard tonight what you know – that Sarah Boden was murdered.'

'Sarah Boden? But what–' He stopped speaking as the shotgun barrel moved again, the muzzle pushing against the right side of his head, moving him away from the lane towards a gap in the hedge. He stumbled through, and the grass was long, soaking his shoes. They were crossing a field, the moonlight whitening the grass in front of him, and they were near the crest of the hill. He shook his head, puzzled. 'I don't understand–'

'If you know Sarah was murdered, you must know more. And if you don't, you're intelligent enough to put all together.'

'The police know she was killed too. It's where I got the information.'

The muzzle wobbled against his shoulder and there was a short silence, broken only by the swishing of the grass under their feet. Then the man behind him sighed. 'All right, you may be telling the truth, though I doubt it, for nothing's appeared in the newspapers. It makes no difference. You'd soon have found out about French.'

'The man from Carlton Engineering?' Ward asked in surprise.

The shotgun muzzle was thrust angrily against his skull. 'You bastard! You know about it all! I was right–'

'No! I only found out he worked for the company this evening! I don't know the significance of it. Except ... except you must have been the man he met in Warkworth.'

'That's right...' The whisper was low, and there was an edge of excitement to it.

'They'll reach you through French, if you were meeting him there. They'll reach you and trace you and fix that murder on you–'

'No. To begin with, French is unlikely to tell them. Too much at stake. I've been keeping him informed regarding the Inland Revenue negotiations so that as soon as the decision is taken to sell the Newfoundland shares, Carlton Engineering, or rather, its parent firm, can step in and take them for a song. You see, my friend, a little bit of industrial espionage has told them that those shares will blow sky-high within the year – an oil-bearing rock offshore – and Morcomb will have unloaded his shares for virtually nothing! That's why French will keep quiet. And even if he didn't, there's no problem. What reason would I have for killing Sarah Boden? Only you and I know that!'

'Me?' Ward shook his head, puzzled. 'I don't know what you're talking about.'

'Don't play me for the fool, Ward.' The shotgun tapped against his back. 'All right, just stand there and turn around. Slowly. Right, hold it there.'

He stood outlined in the moonlight, shadowy through the blurred lenses of Ward's pain-racked eyes, the shotgun pointing straight at Ward's chest. The breeze lifted his hair; the breeze Ward felt at his back. 'Now, slowly,' the man with the shotgun said, 'backwards, one step at a time, slowly.'

'I tell you,' Ward said evenly. 'I've no idea what this is about. You and Sarah Boden—'

'You want to see Lord Morcomb, don't you?' The voice had taken on a grating quality. 'I knew there was something in the air, when you visited Vixen Hill, and when I heard you were going to see Sarah Boden. So when I met French at Warkworth, and saw you come down to dinner, I left, and thought as a matter of curiosity, I'd go to see her. And the silly old bitch told me. And she would have told you...'

Ward understood at last. Sarah Boden had been killed to silence her – the secret she had kept for over twenty years, as an old woman she had been prepared to tell, senility overcoming secrecy. And she had spoken, only to die because of it.

'You won't be seeing Lord Morcomb now, and the past will all be buried. A step more my friend, a step more. The past ... it will all be buried, as soon you will be. An unfortunate accident ... glaucoma ... stumbling in pain in the dark—'

251

'*David!*'

The scream razored through the silence, and the shotgun wavered, turning in an arc, and Eric Ward threw himself forward desperately, his hands thrusting for the gun.

They stood braced against each other in the moonlight, the tall, slimly powerful figure of David Penrose and the thicker, older frame of Eric Ward, the shotgun between them, both men gripping it, barrel and stock. Penrose's finger was on the trigger but Ward's hand was clamped on his and there was only the stamping of their feet and the hissing of their breath to break the silence as Anne Morcomb came running across the grass.

One barrel blazed into the night sky, ineffectually, and then the second roared as Penrose's finger tightened involuntarily against the straining muscles of Ward's body. Ward could see almost nothing; a red agonized haze blurred his vision and shock waves of pain thundered through his head and tore at his eyeballs. Though Penrose was younger than he, and strong, in normal circumstances the roughhousing tactics Ward had learned in the police would have been enough to overcome the man, but the pain debilitated him, robbed him of decision, and made him waver clumsily, struggling to maintain his grip on the shotgun.

The wire caught him at the back of the knees, he felt the scoring pain as iron seared against his thigh and then he was falling backwards, still gripping the shotgun, with Penrose falling with him, half astride him, obscenely struggling to maintain his balance and his upright position. They rolled, and the grass had given way to stone and the night breeze fanned their hot faces. He heard Penrose gasp, felt the grip on the shotgun slacken as Penrose's shoes scrabbled against loose stone and Ward pulled, heaving suddenly at the gun. It came away, Penrose's grip breaking, and almost in the same movement Ward's training reasserted itself and he swung the stock in a short arc.

He felt the stock strike Penrose's jaw with a crunching sound. Penrose moaned softly, and tried to rise, away from Ward's body, and then he slipped sideways on his knees, falling, half conscious.

A moment later, with the sliding rattle of stones, he was gone, with just one single cry, and Eric Ward was alone, on his back in the moonlight, with sharp stones biting into his back.

But not alone. On the other side of the

protective, but broken wire, was Anne Mor-comb.

'Crawl,' she said, half sobbing. 'Eric, for God's sake crawl – but carefully!'

And Eric Ward understood. Half blind, he dragged himself carefully away from the edge of the quarry until the grass was long about him and Anne Morcomb was crying desperately on his shoulder and the nerve-ends around his eyes quivered with the pain that tore relentlessly at them.

She had been in the library, had discussed it with David before he left, then worrying over what Ward had said about Sarah Boden's death, anxious to discover what it had to do with her father, she had heard him come down the stairs. She had heard the front door open and had seen him crossing the lawn. She had run upstairs to don a sweater to follow him, realizing he felt ill, but she had lost him in the darkness of the lane until she saw two dark figures crossing the moonlit field, towards the quarry.

And she had saved his life.

And now here he sat, still pursuing his obsession, as the morning sunshine gleamed through the bedroom window and picked out the pale scalp beneath Lord Morcomb's thinning hair as he sat in his dressing-gown, facing him, slouched in the easy chair. There was a sunken look about his cheeks and his eyes were hollow, but there still gleamed in those eyes a cold defiant light as he stared at Eric Ward.

'I liked that boy. He had no background, but I liked him and I looked after him. And now you say he tried to swindle me.'

'He was a man with an eye for the main chance. He'd been using his inside knowledge of your affairs to feed information to an employee of Carlton Engineering. I suspect, like your financial adviser Henried, that they never really intended to start open-cast mining in the area – that was a bogus pressure, designed to make you sell your shares rather than the land. For that's what they wanted – a sale of Amalgamated Newfoundland Properties, in which Carlton's parent company, Western Consolidated, have a major holding. They wanted to increase it, get a majority holding – and at a low price. It's what they'd have got if you'd unloaded your large holding on to the market. They'd have snapped it up – and paid a handsome fee to Penrose. He kept their man informed of the estate duty negotiations, which were, in a sense, the key. Once the matter was decided, he could tell them the share sales would go through soon. They'd be ready and waiting. And it almost worked.'

'That was hardly enough reason to try to kill you,' Lord Morcomb said carefully. 'Hardly enough reason to die.'

'That wasn't the only reason he attacked me.' Ward held the old man's glance. 'The main reason was Arthur Egan.'

The cold eyes flickered; a tongue touched dry lips. 'What do you mean?'

'When Arthur Egan died he left a sum of money. And a small house. Otherwise, all he kept was a letter, some photographs, a lock of blond hair. Little enough, wasn't it? But he was a lonely man.'

'There'll be some point to this, I trust?' Lord Morcomb said sardonically.

'One of the photographs was of a grave, in Hartbum church.'

The old man's head came up, in a spasm of disbelief. For a moment an old hatred flickered in his eyes, and then it was muffled and gone. He waited.

'The past has a way of always being with us,' Ward said. 'It can influence the present; it can affect the future, and in a manner we never expect. You were married twice, weren't you, Lord Morcomb. Joseph Francis

256

mentioned to me that the first marriage ended with a nullity decree.'

'I don't see–'

'There aren't many grounds on which a nullity decree can be obtained. Certain grounds are laid down by statute – un-soundness of mind, venereal disease and so on. But they weren't the grounds on which your first marriage was nullified, were they?'

Lord Morcomb's head had dropped, chin on chest.

Eric Ward felt a stab of sympathy, but he had to go on for the sake of a dead man he had never met. 'It was incapacity, wasn't it?' he said quietly. 'Not wilful refusal. I think your wife obtained a nullity decree because of your incapacity to consummate the marriage.'

'This has nothing to do with you,' Lord Morcomb grated.

'But it helps me fit all the pieces together. I should have gone out to Hartburn sooner. But when I did go last weekend, and saw the grave, it all came together for me. Vixen Hill, a lock of blond hair, twenty thousand pounds, Fred Bridges's attitude, it all slotted together when I saw that tombstone. Elizabeth Morcomb's grave!'

The old man stirred fretfully. He struggled

to a more upright position, and glared angrily at Eric Ward.

'So she was buried at Hartburn. It was where she was born! There is no reason–'

'But Arthur Egan had taken a photograph of that grave – and kept it by him through all his lonely years at Westerhope! Why did he do that? Why did he accept the trumped-up charge against him for the murder of Colonel Denby? Where did that twenty thousand pounds come from? Who put pressure on the police to get Egan put away? Why did he return, almost as soon as he was released, to hang about Vixen Hill? They are questions that have bothered me, puzzled me – but they were as soon as I saw the grave of your second wife, Anne's mother.'

'This is a lot of nonsense and I–'

'Because it explains also his reluctance, his reticence, right at the end. He was dying, he wanted to make sure his child was financially secure. But he didn't name her ... he was torn. To name her was wrong, and yet to leave her unprovided for, in case she *might* be turned away after all these years... In his cancer agony he could hardly think straight, so he left a cryptic note.'

'I don't know what you're talking about.'

'I'm telling you,' Ward said evenly, '*that I*

know Arthur Egan was Anne's father – not you!'
Lord Morcomb's hand shook. His eyes were fixed on Eric Ward, denying the truth of what he said, but at the same time the past was sweeping over him in a great passionate wave of anger, and hate, and the urge to possess, the drive to destroy. He wanted to deny what Ward asserted, but the urge to explain it after all these years was greater. 'All right!' he almost shouted. 'But do you *understand?* Motives – the tangled web of deceit we were caught up in? When I married Elizabeth I loved her. I loved her and I thought it would be all right. It wasn't my fault I...' He shook his head in a vague desperation. 'How can it be explained? The doctors told me it was nothing physical ... merely psychological. *Merely* psychological! Elizabeth understood; she was sympathetic at first, and for a few years... But then she got moody, depressed, unhappy. But there was nothing I could do, and we began to drift apart.' He fell silent, contemplating the past, hardly aware of Eric Ward's presence.

'And then Arthur Egan came along.'

Lord Morcomb nodded, slowly. His voice was a husky whisper. 'I don't know how it started. She used to ride, a favourite ride past Seddon Burn. And he looked after the stables there – a stable hand, for God's sake!' The lash of hurt pride came back to him momentarily, but subsided again. 'And at last she came to me, told me she had been having an affair with this man Egan, that she was bearing his child and wanted to leave with him.' He looked up, his eyes no longer cold, but burning angrily now. 'I saw Egan. He was *nothing*. A well-set young man, good-looking but he could offer her nothing – except that one thing I could not. Sexual love. So I talked to her, I told her exactly how it would be for her, living with this man in virtual poverty. But she was stubborn – said she loved him...'

'And was it then that you put pressure on Detective-Superintendent Starling?' Eric Ward asked softly.

A spasm of pain crossed Lord Morcomb's lined face. It might have been physical; Ward suspected it was the agony of memory. The old man shook his head. 'It wasn't like that. I heard the rumours; I saw Starling; he said Egan was suspected of the break-in at Vixen Hill, so ... so I told him a conviction would be to both our advantage.'

'And in the end, it was certainly to Starling's advantage,' Ward said. 'Your influence brought him back as Chief Constable years later, I've no doubt. And now he's farming at

Jedburgh. You'll have helped him with his capital, of course...'

The old man's mouth twisted. 'All right, but he told me he thought Egan was guilty, there was evidence ... and then more was unearthed–'

'Lord Morcomb, I believe Egan was innocent. He was just protecting his half-brother!'

'No, I cannot believe that! If I had thought that–'

'Don't try to tell me you would even have been interested! Even if the facts had stared you in the face you would have been blind to them; you wouldn't have wanted to know! You've been afflicted with a certain, deliberate blindness towards Egan all these years. Even if you'd *known,* you would still have *persuaded* Starling to get a conviction,' Ward said harshly. 'Face the facts, for God's sake! You were responsible! You as good as put him in prison – because it suited you. What did you say to Elizabeth, pregnant as she was? Did you say that it was not just a lifetime of working-class drudgery that faced her – but a life with a suspected murderer? Was that how you persuaded her to give him up – and condemn him to a life of loneliness?'

'No, damn you,' Lord Morcomb said, flaring. 'It wasn't like that! She'd already seen sense! Egan's conviction was merely the final straw!'

And Eric Ward now understood how it had been, how it was that Egan had raised no hand in his own defence. There was the dilemma of saving his half-brother, but there was the additional realization that the woman he loved, who was carrying his child, was prepared to give him up for the material things her husband could give her. That was why Egan had accepted his fate without a struggle: he simply didn't care any longer. He had been beaten, dulled, the heart torn out of him by her betrayal. Prison offered no hurt for him; he was hurt enough. He stared at Lord Morcomb, and said, 'But how could you take her back, the way it was? Why was it so important?'

Lord Morcomb's eyes glittered. 'My uncle and I ... we didn't get on. There was talk after the nullity decree that he would pass me the title only, that his own holdings would be left to the damned bog-robbing Irish branch of the family. I couldn't accept that! And when I heard that Elizabeth was pregnant ... you see, my uncle had a sense of family continuity. If I could say my wife was bearing a child I knew his attitude would change. And when I explained it to Elizabeth, she weighed it all in the balance. A life of poverty with a man presently charged with murder, or for her child, possession of the Morcomb estates in their entirety. That's why she gave up Egan – for her child!'

The sun touched his face with a shaft of light, emphasizing the pallor of his skin. 'And that's what happened. Egan was convicted – but I swear I thought... And the child was born, my uncle was delighted, he made a new will ... and then a few years later, Elizabeth died.'

'Anne was about six years old when Arthur Egan came out of prison,' Ward said.

Lord Morcomb smiled grotesquely. 'So you know about that too. Bridges said you'd been asking questions. Yes ... Egan came out, changed, quieter, resigned but he wanted to see his daughter. She used to go over to Vixen Hill in those days, often spending days, and nights, with Michael Denby's aunt. She was happy there – happier than with me here, for there was no woman... I don't know how Egan found out, but he started going into the woods above Vixen Hill, watching for her. Just wanting to see her, perhaps – but Bridges caught him, brought him to me as a poacher. I was terrified, I thought he'd talk to the girl ... and she was mine now, I'd grown to love her... Do you understand that?'

Ward nodded. He understood. 'So you told him how much you could do for the girl, and how little he could do for her. You told him to go away – let you bring her up as yours, give her all the benefits of your wealth and position. And you paid him, didn't you? You paid him, twenty thousand pounds, to go away and leave you both alone. Just, effectively, as you paid Elizabeth by promising her that her child would succeed to the Morcomb estates.'

'All right!' Lord Morcomb coughed, his hand to his mouth as a paroxysm shook him. 'All right,' he wheezed triumphantly, 'but your precious Egan took the damned money, didn't he? He took it, as good as sold her to me!'

Ward shook his head. 'No. You're wrong. Like Elizabeth, he sacrificed his own feelings for his daughter's future. He took the money, but he never spent it. It was this that brought me into the whole case. You see, he left a note saying he wanted the money to go to his child – Anne. He never trusted you, Lord Morcomb, and that money was for her, in case you failed her. He never trusted you – but he had no cause to feel otherwise.'

The old man leaned back in his chair, glaring at Eric Ward. His bony hands gripped the arms fiercely. 'Well, Mr Ward. So you know these things. So why do you have them out with me now? What satisfaction do you get from it all?'

'Don't you understand?' Ward asked softly. 'Egan was a human being – and he was wronged. You sent him – or were instrumental in sending him – to prison for a crime he did not commit. You destroyed the only loving relationship he ever had and you left him with nothing. And when he came out of prison you even made sure he never saw his daughter till he died. You left him nothing, old man, *nothing at all.*'

'It was for the best,' Lord Morcomb said harshly.

'No. Elizabeth remained unhappy until she died. Were you happy? Egan was lonely, embittered, little more than a recluse after you paid him his money and fixed him up with a job through Bridges, far enough away from Sedleigh Hall. And all this web of deceit and lies led to another two deaths – Sarah Boden, and David Penrose.'

'You can't hold me responsible–'

'No, not directly. But Penrose would never have reacted so violently towards me simply had I known about his relationship with French of Carlton Engineering. He needed to kill me because he knew I'd finally work out that he murdered Sarah Boden.'

'But *that* killing – what did it have to do with me, and the past?' Lord Morcomb asked, his face ashen.

'David Penrose was a main chancer. He intended getting money from Carlton Engineering on the side, but he had a bigger prospect in view. Marriage to Anne.'

'I don't–'

'You must have known it. She was hesitating, but he was fairly confident. But he was puzzled by your reaction to the name Egan that first day I came here. And later, Anne told him she'd advised me to see Sarah Boden. So, curious, he went to see her. And was horrified by the story the senile old woman came out with. She had worked at Seddon Burn; she'd previously worked here. She must have seen your wife and Egan together – but had kept quiet all these years. Maybe you paid her to, I don't know. It doesn't matter. But when she spilled the story to him he was horrified. What if the story got out? He was no lawyer. He knew the details of your predecessor's will – maybe he thought the phrase "the heirs of your body" had some legal significance – for he had now learned Anne was not the child of your body. He wouldn't have known that the laws of evidence would prevent the bastardizing of issue in this manner – he just felt that if he didn't stop this babbling old woman's mouth Anne could lose her right to the Morcomb estates. And with that would go his own hopes of a brilliant marriage.' Ward paused, eyeing Lord Morcomb, shrunken in his chair. 'Maybe he didn't intend killing her at first; maybe she did slip and hurt herself. But he sure as hell made certain she wouldn't rise again!'

Actions and events rooted in the past had brought about the deaths of David Penrose and Sarah Boden. The charges against Arthur Egan had, in effect, led to a murder twenty years later, and a violent death at the quarry. And yet, as Ward stared at the old man slumped in the chair, weighed down by the guilts brought home to him, he recognized that there had been a certain desperate inevitability about it all. The people who had lived out those days, all those years ago, could have acted in no other manner than the way they did – Elizabeth Morcomb, passionate but frustrated; Arthur Egan, in love for the only time in his life but betrayed, and careless thereafter; Starling, and Arkwright, and Tiggy Williams, all responding to pressures put upon them; and Lord Morcomb himself – torn by the knowledge of his own his wife's infidelity, savaged by the pride that kept her tied to his side, overcome by the drive that demanded he make the Morcomb estates his own, as one. They could not have acted otherwise than they did, any of them, for that was the way they were made.

As now, Eric Ward could act in no other way than his character and emotions dictated.

She was waiting in the hallway when he came down the stairs. She asked him, and he told her the truth, and her eyes were misty, for the father she loved who was dying, and for the father she had never known who was dead. In a little while she asked him what would happen about all the men who had conspired to send Arthur Egan to prison and he told her it was too long ago; the proofs would never come to hand, and they would now live out their lives and their careers untouched. He explained that the estate of Arthur Egan would go to the Crown as *bona vacantia*, for Tommy Andrews was probably dead, and there were no official heirs of Arthur Egan.

And she asked him what she should do, and he explained about the shares, how she should undertake a balanced divesting across the portfolio and thus prevent the Carlton machinations taking effect.

The police were coming down from the quarry then, as he told her to run the estate, accept her responsibilities and discharge them. There was another, deeper question in her eyes, but he would not let her ask it. He was twenty years older than she, and it was time to say goodbye.

The publishers hope that this book has given you enjoyable reading. Large Print Books are especially designed to be as easy to see and hold as possible. If you wish a complete list of our books please ask at your local library or write directly to:

Magna Large Print Books
Magna House, Long Preston,
Skipton, North Yorkshire.
BD23 4ND

This Large Print Book, for people
who cannot read normal print,
is published under the auspices of

THE ULVERSCROFT FOUNDATION

... we hope you have enjoyed this book.
Please think for a moment about those
who have worse eyesight than you ...
and are unable to even read or enjoy
Large Print without great difficulty.

You can help them by sending a
donation, large or small, to:

**The Ulverscroft Foundation,
1, The Green, Bradgate Road,
Anstey, Leicestershire, LE7 7FU,
England.**
or request a copy of our brochure for
more details.

The Foundation will use all donations
to assist those people who are visually
impaired and need special attention
with medical research, diagnosis
and treatment.

Thank you very much for your help.